P9-CRA-370

NICK AND TESLA'S

SECRET AGENT
GADGET BATTLE

Also Available:

Nick and Tesla's

High-Voltage Danger Lab

Nick And Tesla's

Robot Army Rampage

NICK AND TESLA'S

SECRET AGENT
GADGET BATTLE

A MYSTERY WITH
SPY CAMERAS, CODE WHEELS,
AND OTHER GADGETS YOU CAN
BUILD YOURSELF

BY "SCIENCE BOB"
PFLUGFELDER AND
STEVE HOCKENSMITH

ILLUSTRATIONS BY

SCOTT GARRETT

Copyright © 2014 by Quirk Productions, Inc.

All rights reserved. No part of this book may be reproduced in any form without written permission from the publisher.

Library of Congress Cataloging in Publication Number: 2013911823

ISBN: 978-1-59474-676-5

Printed in China
Typeset in Caecilia, Futura, and Russell Square

Designed by Doogie Horner
Illustrations by Scott Garrett
Production management by John J. McGurk

Quirk Books
215 Church Street
Philadelphia, PA 19106
quirkbooks.com

10 9 8 7 6 5 4 3 2 1

DANGER! DANGER! DANGER! DANGER!

The how-to projects in this book involve motors, hydraulic power, hot glue, booby traps, and other potentially dangerous elements. Before you build any of the projects, ASK AN ADULT TO REVIEW THE INSTRUCTIONS. You'll probably need their help with one or two of the steps, anyway.

While we believe these projects to be safe and family-friendly, accidents can happen in any situation, and we cannot guarantee your safety. THE AUTHORS AND PUBLISHER DISCLAIM ANY LIABILITY FROM ANY HARM OR INJURY THAT MAY RESULT FROM THE USE, PROPER OR IMPROPER, OF THE INFORMATION CONTAINED IN THIS BOOK. Remember, the instructions in this book are not meant to be a substitute for your good judgment and common sense.

CHAPTER

1

"It's her," Nick said. "She's the spy."

"Who is?" said Tesla.

She looked around. She and her brother were in their uncle's backyard, about to test-fly the hoop glider they'd been working on that morning. There was only one other person in sight: a fortyish woman crouched over a bed of begonias about forty feet away. She was wearing jeans and a T-shirt and dirty gardening gloves. A sweat-soaked bandana was wrapped around her head.

She didn't look much like a spy to Tesla.

"You mean Julie Casserly?"

Nick nodded, eyeing the woman suspiciously.

"I can feel it in my gut," he said. "She's always watching us. Always glaring."

"Well, of course she is. Wouldn't you if you lived next door to Uncle Newt?"

Nick and Tesla's uncle was an inspired, ingenious, innovative inventor. Unfortunately, he was also a forgetful, dreamy, not-particularly-safety-minded one. Since the kids had come to stay with him a couple weeks earlier, his out-of-control creations had chewed up Julie's flower beds, demolished one of her garden gnomes, set her lawn on fire, and splattered her car with thirty pounds of putrid bananas flambé. (Uncle Newt was convinced he could build an engine for a vacuum cleaner that ran on compost. So far, he'd only succeeded in building several extremely smelly time bombs.)

Maybe Julie would have overcome her dislike for Uncle Newt and warmed up to Nick and Tesla— *maybe*—but the kids were wannabe inventors themselves. They could often be found in their uncle's backyard testing out homemade hovercrafts and balloon rockets and robots.

And, this day, a hoop glider.

"What is that?" Julie said when Tesla lifted the glider and prepared to send it on its first flight. She'd turned from her begonias to shoot Nick and Tesla a wary glare. "A remote-controlled spear?"

Tesla lowered the glider. It was just a couple hoops of stiff paper, a small one in front and a larger one behind it, connected by a straw.

"No," said Tesla.

"A computerized javelin?" said Julie.

"No."

"A self-shooting arrow?"

"No."

"Some kind of missile?"

"No."

"It's a glider," said Nick.

Julie narrowed her eyes. "And what's that supposed to do?"

"Uhh . . . glide," said Tesla.

Julie cocked her head, her lips twisting into a tight, sarcastic smile.

"Oh, sure. It just glides," she said. She pushed herself up from her knees and began walking away. "Well, let me get inside before you set it loose. I don't

want to be here when it 'glides' someone into the hospital."

The woman marched around the corner of her house and disappeared.

"Not very brave for a spy," Tesla said.

"Maybe that's just her cover," Nick grumbled. "Anyway, go ahead. I want to see if this thing works."

Tesla brought the glider up again, pointed it away from Julie's yard, and launched it with a flick of the wrist. It shot away with surprising speed and flew smoothly over Uncle Newt's lawn, arcing to the left as it went.

"Whoa! Look at it go!" said Nick.

"And go and go and go," said Tesla.

She'd expected the glider to fly five yards, tops, yet even after twenty it was still six feet off the ground and not slowing down. In fact, it was soaring toward some trees on the other side of Uncle Newt's property, perhaps about to fly out of the yard altogether.

"Hey, kids!" a cheerful voice called out. "Whatcha up to?"

It was Uncle Newt's other neighbor, Mr. Jones, stepping out onto his patio. The paunchy, gray-haired man was wary of Uncle Newt's inventions—which was wise—yet he always had a smile and a wave for Nick and Tesla.

Unfortunately, it was a really bad time for a smile and a wave.

"Mr. Jones!" Nick cried out. "Duck!"

"A duck? Where?"

Mr. Jones looked up into the sky.

The glider came swooping through the trees and smacked him in the face.

Nick and Tesla ran to the old man as he staggered back into his house. He managed to find his footing again just as the kids reached him.

"Where did that crazy duck go?" he started to say.

Then he saw the hoop glider lying in the doorway.

"Oh," he said.

"We're sorry, Mr. Jones," said Nick.

"We had no idea it was going to fly this far," said Tesla.

Mr. Jones rubbed his bulbous nose—which was now slightly more bulbous and *way* redder than usual.

"No harm done," he said.

He didn't sound like he meant it, though, and the smile he gave the kids when he handed them their glider seemed strained.

Mr. Jones closed the door on Nick and Tesla, muttering something about getting an ice pack.

"Great," Tesla said as she and her brother trudged away. "The one neighbor who's nice, and we go and throw a paper airplane up his nose."

"It was an accident," Nick said. "And who's to say Mr. Jones is such a nice guy anyway?"

"What?"

Tesla looked over at her brother, thinking he might be joking.

Nick hadn't been joking much lately, though. And he *never* joked about this.

"It's him," Nick said. "He's the spy."

"Mr. Jones? He must be, like, two hundred years old."

"Spies get old like everyone else." Nick threw a suspicious squint over his shoulder. "He's always watching us. Always smiling."

"So now being nice makes someone a suspect?"

"Why not? You remember what Mom said."

Tesla did remember, of course.

She just *wished* she could forget.

Nick and Tesla were supposed to go to Disneyland. They were supposed to take tennis lessons. They were supposed to see movies that were 99 percent special effects and explosions. They were supposed to drink too much Kool-Aid and go swimming at the local pool and hang out with their friends.

They were supposed to have a normal summer.

Instead, they'd ended up with their uncle and were having the weirdest summer ever.

Their parents were scientists—agriculture experts for the government—and two days after school let out they were suddenly ordered to Uzbekistan to study amazing advances in soybean farming. Or so they said before putting Nick and Tesla on the plane to California, where the kids would be staying with an eccentric uncle they barely knew. After that, two weeks went by without a word from Nick and Tesla's mom and dad.

Then the message came. A voicemail from their mother.

"Tesla! Nick! There's so much I want to tell you, but there's no time! Everything's more . . . complicated than we led you to believe. We sent you to your uncle to keep you safe. But you're not. The people we were trying to hide you from know where you are. They might even be there already. Whatever you do, don't trust—"

Then static, then a beep. Then silence.

Nick and Tesla played the message again and again and again. And when their uncle got home, they tried to play it *again*. Only this time, instead of hearing "Nick! Tesla! There's so much I want to tell you," they heard this, intoned in a robotic drone:

"No new messages."

"What?" yelped Nick, gaping at the phone in his hand as if it had just bitten him.

"You must have hit the wrong button," said Tesla.

"I didn't! I'm positive!"

Nick began punching numbers on the keypad, hurrying through the voicemail options.

Uncle Newt yawned. It was late, and he wanted to go to bed.

"No new messages," the robo-operator said again.

"Oh, no . . . you must have erased it," Tesla said to Nick.

"No, I didn't!" he barked back.

"Maybe by accident."

"No way!"

"Then what happened to it?"

Nick thought a moment. Then his eyes went wide.

"Of course," he said. "*He* erased it."

"He?"

"Or she."

"She?"

"Or them."

"Them? What are you talking about?"

"What do you think? *The spies!*"

"Huh? Who? What?" said Uncle Newt, jerking his head up from the dining room table.

He had just meant to rest his eyes and ended up falling asleep. Somehow, he'd instantly acquired a severe case of bed head. His graying hair was always a little wild, but now it looked like he'd stuck his finger in an electrical socket.

"We can't play you the message," Tesla told him. "It got erased."

"Somehow," Nick added ominously.

"Oh, well. Don't worry about it," Uncle Newt said. "You told me the gist of it. 'There's so much to say,' 'things are complicated,' 'don't talk to strangers,' yada yada yada. That's just the way mothers talk."

"*What?*" Nick said in disbelief.

"Sure. Your grandmother used to leave me messages like that all the time. 'Don't forget to eat.' 'If you won't do laundry, at least buy new underwear.' 'Maybe you shouldn't keep all that industrial waste in your basement.' Such a worrywart. Like all moms."

Uncle Newt suddenly perked up and cocked his head, as if he'd heard something disturbing outside.

"What is it?" Nick said.

"I just remembered," said Uncle Newt. "I need to buy new underwear."

He stood and walked toward the stairs to the second floor.

He was going to bed.

"Uncle Newt, really," Tesla said. "Mom sounded upset. And she definitely implied we're in danger."

"She didn't *imply* it!" Nick protested. "She said it!"

"All right, all right." Uncle Newt changed course, spinning on his heel until he was facing the back of the house. "I'll make sure the doors and windows are locked, and I'll activate the home security system. If anyone gets through all that, they'll have to contend with my vicious attack cat."

"Gee," said Tesla. "Thanks."

The "home security system" was the light on the back porch. (The light on the front porch was burned out.) And Uncle Newt's "vicious attack cat," Eureka, was hairless, wrinkled, and not known to attack anything other than whatever food he could drag off the kitchen counter. Tesla had once watched the cat ignore an entire family of mice darting across the floor because he was too busy mauling a jelly doughnut.

"Sleep tight!" Uncle Newt said as he started up the stairs a moment later.

"Yeah," Nick said. "Right."

That night, Nick did not sleep tight. He did not sleep loose. He did not really sleep at all. Instead he tossed and turned and stewed on one question: *Who?*

As he ran through his list of suspects—an extremely short list, since he and Tesla knew only a dozen people in town—he toyed with the star-shaped pendant hanging around his neck. His parents had given one to him and one to Tesla the day before they sent them off to California. Nick suspected the pendants were tracking devices. Which raised another question: *Why?* A couple plant scientists run off to watch beans grow on the other side of the world, but before they go they hang homing beacons on their kids? It didn't make sense. Not if anything Nick and Tesla thought they knew about their parents was true . . .

Tesla had a slightly easier time letting go of her worries and getting some rest. She'd always been bolder than her brother, something she attributed to her greater age and experience.

Nick was eleven years, five months, two weeks, six days, twenty hours, and fifteen minutes old.

Tesla was eleven years, five months, two weeks, six days, twenty hours, and twenty-seven minutes old.

For twelve minutes she'd been an only child, and that kind of experience really toughens a person.

Not that Tesla was immune to fear. Only a fool would be unconcerned after that message from their mother. (Which didn't reflect especially well on Uncle Newt.) But what could she and her brother do except keep their guard up and their heads down?

It would be up to the people their parents were hiding them from—whoever they were—to make the first move.

Tesla awoke with a start. A dark shape was looming over her bed in the gray morning light.

She balled a fist and got ready to punch it.

"It's Sergeant Feiffer," said the dark shape—Nick. "He's the spy."

"Geez, thanks for the scare," Tesla groaned, fighting the urge to go ahead and use the fist on him. "How long have you been watching me like that?"

"Just five or ten minutes," Nick said. "Did you know you snore when you sleep on your back?"

"No. I didn't know. Because I was asleep. Which is how I'd still like to be."

Tesla turned on her side and closed her eyes.

After a few seconds, she flopped onto her back again.

Nick was still hovering over her bed.

"Did you say Sergeant Feiffer's a spy?" she asked him.

Sergeant Feiffer was the town's one and only cop. Nick and Tesla had done his job for him on a couple occasions, catching kidnappers and a local thief. So he didn't strike Tesla as especially competent. He didn't seem especially sinister either.

Nick nodded, though.

"He's the person Mom was telling us not to trust," Nick said. "I can feel it in my gut."

"Does your gut have any proof?"

"No. But doesn't it make sense? He's it when it comes to local law enforcement. If the bad guys had him in their pocket, we'd be at their mercy."

"Just because it makes sense doesn't make it true," Tesla pointed out. "I mean, wouldn't it make just as much sense if the mailman were the spy? He's here practically every day. It'd be the perfect way to keep an eye on us."

"Whoa," Nick said. "You're right!"

"That was just an example, Nick. I don't really think the mailman's a spy."

"But what if he is? He's always looking at us if we're in the yard when he comes with the mail. Waving at us. Saying 'How ya doing?'"

"Very suspicious."

Tesla rolled her eyes.

Nick didn't notice.

"I know," he said. "Isn't it?"

"Argh!"

Tesla launched herself out of bed.

"Do you know what I can feel in my gut?" she said as she stomped off toward the door.

"What?"

"Nothing."

And she headed downstairs for breakfast.

When Nick came down to the dining room a minute later, he was able to admit that he was being silly. It was ridiculous to think the mailman might be a spy.

Especially, he said, when the real spy was obviously Uncle Newt's new lady friend, Dr. Hiroko Sakurai.

If Tesla hadn't been enjoying her Pop-Tart so much, she would've thrown it at him.

"Just think about it," Nick said when he saw the look on his sister's face. "She just showed up in town, like, a week ago and suddenly she's hanging around with Uncle Newt all the time?"

Nick waved a hand at the dusty old computers piled up in a corner, the ancient diving suit and telescope and stuffed polar bear in the hall, the brown-needled Christmas tree that stayed lit 24-7 even though it was nearly July. Wires protruded from holes in the wall here and there, and the floor was littered with abandoned circuit boards and actuators and science journals and bunches of gnat-covered bananas (which weren't *quite* black enough for Uncle Newt's compost engine yet).

"Let's face it," Nick said. "Our uncle's not exactly a catch."

"That doesn't make Hiroko a spy."

"And that doesn't make her *not* a spy."

"What kind of logic is that?"

"The we-know-somebody's-after-us-but-we-don't-know-who-so-we-shouldn't-be-too-trusting kind."

"Paranoia, in other words."

Nick mulled that over.

"I prefer to think of it as justifiable suspicion," he said. "Of everyone."

Tesla sighed.

"I know what you need," she said.

"Bodyguards?"

"No. A distraction."

If there was one thing Nick liked to do more than worry, it was build stuff. Cool stuff that would do cool things. Tesla felt the same way, which was why their uncle's basement laboratory wasn't packed with just *his* experiments. The kids were always trying out new ideas, too.

The hoop glider was pretty simple, by their standards, but that was why it was perfect. Tesla wanted something they could build fast, before Nick could start obsessing about spies again, and it might help to get him outside, too. It was a gorgeous northern California day, sunny yet cool thanks to the steady breeze coming off the ocean half a mile away.

"Beautiful," Tesla said, smiling up at the cloudless blue sky.

"Is that a drone?" said Nick, frowning up at a distant black dot that was probably just a crow.

Tesla scowled at him.

"Come on," she said, leading her brother out into the yard. A minute later, after their not-so-neighborly chat with Julie Casserly, Tesla was launching the glider, which promptly swooped out of Uncle Newt's yard and bopped Mr. Jones on the nose.

"I'm telling you," Nick said as they walked back to Uncle Newt's house. "Mr. Jones is the spy. I can feel it in my gut."

"You know, I wish you and your dumb gut would shut up!" Tesla snapped. "Is there anyone you *don't* think is a spy?"

A squirrel scampered across the lawn.

Tesla pointed at it.

"Watch out! A spy!"

"Come on, Tez. I'm not being *that* bad."

A car honked in the distance. Tesla cupped a hand to her ear.

"Hark! A spy!"

"Okay, okay, I get it. I'm going overboard."

Tesla pointed at herself. "Oh, my gosh! Right next to you! Spy!"

"Geez, Tez—I said I get it."

Tesla smiled.

"Good. I know that message was scary, but there's nothing to freak out about. I'm sure things aren't nearly as bad as they sounded. I mean, what kind of spy's going to waste his time on a couple eleven-year-olds?"

Nick nodded glumly, looking unconvinced.

Tesla wasn't convinced either, but she'd decided not to show it.

"Now let's get a new straw for the glider and try it again," she said. "And no more obsessing about spies. Deal?"

"Deal," Nick mumbled.

He and Tesla crossed the patio and went through

the back door into Uncle Newt's kitchen.

A huge man in a trench coat and fedora was waiting for them. In his right hand he was holding something long and shiny and sharp.

"So we meet at last," the man said in a deep voice with a heavy accent. "I have questions for you two. For your sake, I hope you have the right answers."

"Tez?" Nick said under his breath. "Deal's off."

CHAPTER

2

The long, shiny, sharp thing the man was holding was a knife.

With a big glob of peanut butter on it.

"Where is jelly?" the man said.

"Jelly?" said Nick.

"Yes! And milk."

"Milk?" said Tesla.

The man nodded so vigorously his hat almost fell off.

"Yes! I am finding loaf of the bread and butter of the peanut, but not jelly or milk. Sticks of the carrot I am also not finding."

"Sticks of the carrot?" said Nick.

The man nodded again. He

had a round, stubble-covered face and big eyes that bulged as he spoke.

"Yes! Or stalks of the celery. How am I to make nutritious lunch for youngsters without these things? All I am seeing in your kitchen is can of this, box of that. Bah! You must eat hearty, *fresh* food if you are to grow up big and healthy and strong like Oli."

"Oli?" said Tesla.

The man slapped his broad chest with his free hand.

"Yes! Oli! From M.A.D.S.!"

"M.A.D.S.?" Nick said.

Tesla decided that simply repeating things the man said with a question mark was getting them nowhere.

"Hold on," she broke in. "Who the heck are you?"

The man looked puzzled and a little hurt. Before he could answer Tesla's question, Uncle Newt came up the stairs from his basement laboratory. Wisps of smoke came with him, and one side of his lab coat was singed and smoldering.

Apparently, Uncle Newt still hadn't perfected his compost engine.

"Oh, hi, kids!" he said cheerfully as he walked

to the refrigerator. "I see you've met Oli. When he's done fixing you lunch, send him down to the lab. I have some errands for him to run."

He pulled a can of Coke out of the fridge, popped it open, and took a long slurp as he headed back toward the stairwell.

"Uncle Newt," Tesla said, "*who is Oli?*"

"Me!" the man said.

"Yeah," said Uncle Newt. "Him."

He was about to go down the stairs and leave Nick and Tesla alone with the man again.

"Stop!" Nick cried out.

Uncle Newt turned to stare at him.

"Maybe you should introduce Oli to us properly," Nick said. "You know . . . tell us why he's here?"

"Oh. Okay," Uncle Newt said. "Oli Whatever-your-lastnameis, meet Nick and Tesla Holt. My nephew and niece. Nick and Tesla Holt, meet Oli Whatever-hislastnameis. My apprentice."

"Apprentice?" Nick said.

Tesla was really sick of the repeating-words-with-a-question-mark thing, but she just couldn't help herself.

"Yeah," she said. "Apprentice?"

"Yes. Apprentice," Uncle Newt said. "From the Multinational Alliance of Developmental Scientists. My union. Apparently, I agreed to have an apprentice for a few months. Oli's going to be living here while I show him how we M.A.D. Scientists get things done."

"Uhhh, Uncle Newt?" said Nick. "Why do you say *apparently* you agreed to have an apprentice?"

Uncle Newt grinned. "Well, you know me! I forgot the whole thing. I didn't remember till Oli knocked on the door a few minutes ago." His grin sagged slightly. "Actually, I didn't even remember about it then. I still don't remember. But hey—I must have signed up for the program, right? Why would anyone show up on my doorstep pretending to be my apprentice? That'd be crazy, right?"

Uncle Newt was chuckling as he continued down the stairs to the basement.

Nick and Tesla weren't.

Why would anyone show up pretending to be Uncle Newt's apprentice? Easy.

To get close to *them*.

"So . . . where were we?" Oli said. "Oh, yes!"

He swiveled toward the kids with the knife still clutched in his hand. The wide brim of his fedora cast a shadow over his eyes, and his expression darkened, turning determined and grim.

"Where is jelly?" he said.

There was no jelly, much to Oli's dismay. There wasn't even any fruit he could mash into jelly other than the bunches of withered brown bananas abandoned here and there around the house and a bag of apricots with FOR EXPERIMENTS ONLY—DON'T EAT!!! scrawled across the label.

"Cocoa Pebbles? Crunch Berries?" Oli muttered indignantly as he rummaged through the shelves. "How can Dr. Newt create the science with food of this kind? A great mind requires great fuel. This is not fuel fit for mind of slug!"

"Maybe that's why Uncle Newt forgot you were coming," Tesla said.

"Yes. Perhaps," Oli said, oblivious to Tesla's sarcasm. "The Beefaroni and the Beanee Weenees—they have taken their toll. *Aha!*"

Oli pulled out a bag of jelly beans and shook them triumphantly.

"These are filled with jelly, yes?" he said. "I will

squeeze the beans for to make your sandwiches."

"Uhh . . . those don't really have jelly in them," Nick said.

"What?" Oli stabbed a finger at the word JELLY on the package. "You are saying this is lie?"

"'Jelly beans' is just what they're called," Tesla said. "It's like 'hot dogs.' No one thinks they're made out of dogs."

Oli gaped at her.

"Hot dogs are not made out of—?"

He cut himself off and tossed the jelly beans back in the cabinet.

"The food here is unsane!" he declared. Then he stomped to the counter and finished making the kids plain "butter of the peanut" sandwiches, which he hacked into quarters with entirely too much relish.

"Here," he said, heaping the sandwich wedges onto plates and thrusting them at the kids. "Nourish yourselves as you can. Later, Oli will make you *real* meal."

Nick and Tesla reluctantly accepted the plates, but neither one touched the food.

"Oli," Tesla said, "why are you wearing that hat

and coat?"

Oli looked down at his trench coat. There was a big dab of peanut butter stuck to one lapel. He wiped it away with a finger, then proceeded to pop it into his mouth. He grimaced slightly, as if he'd never tasted anything like it before and couldn't decide if he should swallow.

"When I learn I am coming to northern California, near San Francisco, I do with the Google." Oli waggled his fingers in the air, miming typing on an invisible keyboard. "It says it can be cold, even in summer. So I dress for chill. Where I am from is always warm."

"Where *are* you from?" Nick asked.

"Australia."

Nick and Tesla looked at each other. It was obvious what needed to be said next.

Tesla raised her hands, palms toward her brother, the gesture saying, "Be my guest."

They turned back to Oli.

"Australia?" Nick said.

"Yes." As an afterthought, Oli added, "Mate."

"That's funny, Oli," Tesla said. "Because you sure don't *sound* like you're from—"

"Do you hear that?" Oli interrupted, cupping a hand to his ear. "Dr. Newt is calling me."

Nick and Tesla listened.

They didn't hear a thing.

"Yes, yes. Your uncle needs me," Oli said. "I must go to him. I am so excited to be learning how to make with the science!"

The big man hustled from the dining room, and a moment later Nick and Tesla heard him clomping down to the basement.

"Well, mystery solved," Nick whispered as soon as he was sure Oli was out of hearing range. "Now the question is, what do we do about it?"

"What do you mean, mystery solved?" Tesla asked.

Nick blinked at her in shock. "The spy Mom warned us about." He jerked a thumb at the doorway Oli had just left through. "I mean . . . duh."

"I don't know," Tesla said. "Doesn't it seem a bit too obvious? The guy might as well have a neon sign around his neck flashing SPY! SPY! SPY!"

"So you don't think he's a spy because he seems too much like a spy?"

"I'm not saying that. It's just that if he *is* a spy, he

must be the worst one in the world."

"Then we should count ourselves lucky! We have an enemy, and he's an idiot. Good for us! It'll be that much easier to stay alive."

Tesla shook her head, still unconvinced.

"Do you really think Mom would have been so worried about someone like Oli?" she said.

"Oh, that's just—!" Nick began indignantly.

His shoulders slumped as what his sister said sunk in.

"—a really good point," he said. "But isn't Oli still the most obvious suspect? It's not like we've had any other mysterious strangers popping up all of a sudden."

The doorbell rang.

Before Nick or Tesla could even get up to go to the door, it was swinging open, and a lean, mustachioed man in a tan jumpsuit came striding into the house. He was holding a long gold nozzle in his hands. A thin hose ran from it to a black pack strapped to his back.

Nick jumped up from the table.

"Fl—?" he said. "Fla—? Flam—!"

The word he was trying to say was *flamethrower*.

The man made an adjustment to the nozzle, and it began hissing slightly.

"I hear there are some little pests around here," the man said. He grinned malevolently. "I'm here to make sure they never bother anyone ever again."

3

Nick ran out of the room screaming.

"Come back!" Tesla shouted after him. "He's an exterminator!"

"I know! I know!" Nick screeched from the kitchen.

"Of *bugs*, Nick!"

Tesla glanced back at the man in the tan jumpsuit just to make sure he wasn't about to send a jet of liquid flame her way.

"That *is* for killing termites, right?" she said, pointing at the sprayer on his back.

"Among other things," the man said. He jerked his chin at the door Nick had just dashed through. "Is that kid all right?"

"He's just been a little stressed out lately, that's all." Tesla turned toward the kitchen again. "Nick! It's all right! I'm still alive!"

Slow, soft footsteps could be heard crossing the kitchen, and then Nick eased his head around the corner.

"You are?" he said.

There were more footsteps, quicker but heavier, and Uncle Newt and Oli appeared behind him.

"What's all the yelling about?" Uncle Newt said. "I haven't blown anything up all day." He looked at the exterminator and grinned. "Ahh! The maid!" His gaze shifted to something behind the man. "And the exterminators, too! What timing!"

Nick and Tesla followed their uncle's gaze and saw a pair of tiny, white-haired women in powder-blue smocks peering into the house through the open front door.

"Maid? Exterminators?" said Nick.

"You mean exterminator," the man in the jump-suit said indignantly, thumping his chest with a thumb, "and maids."

"Right, fine, great, whatever," said Uncle Newt.

He began waving the maids inside. "Come in, come in! You've got the right place!"

The little old ladies looked dubious, but they gathered up the supplies they'd left on the porch behind them—buckets and spray bottles and brooms and mops—and began lugging them inside.

"Uncle Newt," Tesla said, "what is going on?"

"Oh, I was just thinking the place needed a little tidying up. When Hiroko dropped by yesterday, she looked a little put off by the mess. And the gnats. And the brown recluse spider on the dining room table."

"Brown recluse spider!" Nick yelped. "Those things are dangerous!"

"Oh, wait. It wasn't a brown recluse," Uncle Newt said, chuckling at his own foolishness. "They're not native to California."

Nick sighed in relief.

"Silly me," Uncle Newt said. "It was a black widow."

Nick went very, very pale.

"Don't worry," his uncle assured him. "I got it and put it . . . uhh . . . somewhere."

Nick's face didn't regain any color.

"So let me see if I understand," Tesla said. "Nick and I come to live with you, and you don't so much as sweep the floor. But a lady you like maybe notices some dust, and suddenly it's time to call in the professionals?"

Uncle Newt nodded, still grinning obliviously.

"Yup," he said. "Lucky for me I just happened to hear from Maids-to-Order and Verminator Pest Control yesterday. They were both running specials. First day of service is free!"

"Yeah, right," Tesla said, eyeing the exterminator and the maids. "How very lucky."

"Where you want us to start, mister?" said one of the maids.

"Doesn't matter to me," Uncle Newt told her. "You have the run of the house."

"Is that really such a good idea?" Nick said, his gaze sweeping the ceiling for spiders.

Uncle Newt didn't hear him because the man from Verminator Pest Control spoke at the same moment.

"How about me?" he said.

"Oh, just go wherever they're not," Uncle Newt said, waving a hand at the maids. "Now come along,

Oli. You've got a compost combustion chamber to clean out for me."

"And this is science?" Oli asked.

"Of course!" Uncle Newt assured him as they turned and left. "Sort of."

The Verminator guy began wandering around spraying pesticide here and there at random. As he came closer, Tesla noticed a name stitched in curly gold letters over the left breast of his jumpsuit.

Skip

The maids just stood staring around the clutter-filled house with dazed "What have we gotten ourselves into?" looks on their faces.

"Come along, sister," Nick said stiffly. "Let us go outside and 'play' with our 'toys.'"

He wasn't the best actor in the world.

"There you go! *There you go!*" he exploded once he and Tesla were in the backyard. "Is that enough suspects for you? One of those people has *got* to be a spy. Or all of them, for all we know!"

"It is weird how they all showed up the day after we got Mom's message."

"Weird? It's not weird. It's terrifying! Our uncle's house is filled with spies and black widow spiders! Mom and Dad might as well have sent us to live with a family of cobras in a volcano."

"Calm down, Nick. It was one spider, and Uncle Newt caught it. And I can think of an easy way to thwart spies."

"Really? How?"

"Don't give them anything to spy on," Tesla said. She started walking toward the street. "Come on."

"So we just stay away?" Nick said as he hustled after her. "That's only going to work for so long. We'll have to go back eventually."

"I know," Tesla said. "But hopefully when we do go back, we'll have reinforcements."

Uncle Newt lived in a quiet neighborhood sand-wiched by the Pacific Ocean on one side and little downtown Half Moon Bay, California, on the other. Even in the summertime, the ocean was too cold to swim in without a wetsuit, and there wasn't much for kids to do downtown except eat frozen yogurt from the It's-Froze-Yo! (if they had the money for it)

and watch tourists pull in off the Pacific Coast High-way in search of antiques, local color, and nonfat cappuccinos.

So Nick and Tesla knew where to look for their friends Silas and DeMarco. If they weren't cruising the neighborhood on their bikes in the hope that something, *anything* interesting was happening, they'd be in Silas's or DeMarco's backyard *making* something interesting happen.

This day, it was DeMarco's yard. And the something interesting was, apparently, DeMarco's suicide.

Silas was perched at the top of a slide attached to a rickety metal play set, a garden hose in his hands. Water flowed down the slide into a mud pit DeMarco was making even muddier by busting up sod with a shovel.

DeMarco's bicycle was leaning against the ladder leading up to the top of the slide.

"No way," Nick said, instantly grasping what his friends were planning.

DeMarco grinned.

"Yes way," he said.

DeMarco wanted to be a stuntman when he grew up. And if he couldn't find anyone to pay him to crash cars and leap off buildings, he said, then he'd just do it for free.

In the meantime, he liked to do things like jump over mud pits by riding bikes down slicked-up slides.

"Seems pretty tame, actually. There's only a seventy-five percent chance you'll break your neck," Tesla said. "Couldn't you get the hose up on the roof?"

She was being sarcastic.

Silas didn't notice.

"The roof's been off-limits since the time DeMarco broke his collarbone, so we're making this a little more interesting," he said from the top of the slide. He was a big kid—a soon-to-be eighth grader who looked like he was ready for college. It was a bit of a miracle that the slide wasn't crumpling beneath him.

"Does your mom know you're doing this?" Nick asked DeMarco.

DeMarco planted the shovel in the mud and leaned against it. He was so short and lean he didn't seem much bigger than the shovel.

"I don't think she'll complain as long as it keeps me safe and sound in the backyard."

Nick watched water pour down DeMarco's makeshift ramp.

"*This* is safe and sound?"

"Compared to some things," DeMarco said.

He waggled his eyebrows at Tesla.

"What?" she said. "*Us? We're* dangerous?"

DeMarco shrugged.

"According to my mom and dad."

"They're pretty down on you two right now," Silas explained. "They say you're trouble."

"We're not trouble!" Tesla protested. "We just lead interesting lives."

DeMarco laughed at the understatement.

"So tell me," he said, "what's going on over at your uncle's today?"

"Trouble," said Nick.

Tesla shot him a frown.

"Well, it's true!" Nick said. And he went on to tell Silas and DeMarco about their mother's warning and the sudden appearance of four potential spies: Oli the "apprentice," Skip the Verminator, and the maids.

"Too bad you can't just call Agent McIntyre with your little thingamajigs," Silas said, pointing down at the pendant that hung around Nick's neck.

Agent McIntyre was a mysterious friend of Nick and Tesla's parents. She'd shown up to help the kids once before, but they had no idea how to contact her. They'd once tried simply screaming into the pendants, but it soon became obvious that whatever the little star-shaped "thingamajigs" were, they weren't walkie-talkies.

"Well, Agent McIntyre's not around," Tesla said. "Uncle Newt is, but he's . . . you know. Uncle Newt. So we're on our own."

"Maybe you guys could come over and help us spy on the spies," Nick suggested.

"Ooo! Cool!" Silas said.

DeMarco looked unenthused, though.

"If they even are spies," he said. "Seems more like we'd just end up spying on some cleaning ladies, a bug guy, and a dude with a weird thing for peanut butter and jelly."

"You don't believe us?" Nick asked, incredulous. "About the message from our mom?"

"It's not that I don't believe you. It's just that—"

"He's scared," Tesla said.

DeMarco snapped up to his full (diminutive) height and glared at Tesla across the gloppy, ever-expanding mud puddle at his feet.

"I am not scared of any of your so-called spies," he said.

"I know," Tesla replied. "It's your parents you're scared of. And your sisters."

DeMarco's mouth puckered into a small, hard line. It was obvious he wanted to deny what Tesla had said . . . and just as obvious that he couldn't.

DeMarco was the oldest kid in his house, but not even remotely close to the meanest.

DeMarco lived for thrills. His sisters lived to get him in trouble.

"We understand," Nick said. "We'll just have to figure out something else. Come on, Tez."

Nick and his sister turned to leave.

"Wait!" Silas called out. "Maybe I can YEEEEEEEE!"

The *YEEEEEEEE!* ended in a *SPLOOSH!*

Silas had slipped and slid down the slide. When his 170 pounds hit the ground, an equal amount of mud spurted out in all directions.

Somehow, most of it managed to land on Nick and Tesla. Gooey brown glop covered them from head to toe.

Silas lifted his face from the sludge, spat out a

mouthful of muck, and said, "Sorry."

DeMarco burst out laughing. He'd been just as close to the puddle as Nick and Tesla, yet he was totally clean except for a single, small streak on his jeans.

"Thanks," Tesla spat at him. She swung her furious glare over to Silas. "Thanks for everything. I knew we could count on you."

She spun on her heel—which was easy to do, considering how slick with sludge it was—and stomped off.

"Oh, come on, Tez!" Silas moaned. "It was an accident!"

Tesla didn't look back.

"If a few days go by and you haven't seen us," Nick said, "call the police."

He turned and set off after his sister, his soaked shoes squishing with every step.

Uncle Newt's house had only one usable shower. (There were two bathtubs, but one was filled with the leftovers from a failed attempt to grow glow-in-the-dark mushrooms.) So either Nick or Tesla was going to have to wait while the other got clean.

"I'll pay two million dollars for dibs on the bathroom," Tesla said as she and her brother tracked ooze across the neighborhood.

"Four million dollars," said Nick. "And keep your shower short."

"Deal."

Nick and Tesla did a lot of big-money wheeling and dealing. Thanks to this newest bargain, Nick's debt to his sister was now down to nine million dollars. He fully intended to pay her, too—if he ever had any money.

When they got to the house, Tesla kicked off her shoes and went inside while Nick waited on the back porch. After a few seconds, there was a shriek from inside, but Nick knew Tesla wasn't in trouble.

It sounded like one of the cleaning ladies. Nick didn't blame the woman for screaming. Even with her shoes off, Tesla was probably leaving a soggy brown trail through the house, and she and Nick were so coated in mud they looked like a couple Sasquatches (albeit not particularly tall ones).

While Nick waited, he noticed Julie Casserly installing a new garden gnome by the bushes beside her house. (Its predecessor had been destroyed when one of Uncle Newt's inventions—a supposedly self-controlled lawn mower—got snagged on it and blew up.)

"Let me guess," Julie said when she noticed Nick watching her. "A harmless little experiment didn't go as planned."

Nick shook his head. The mud covering him had begun to dry under the summer sun, and big, crumbly chunks flaked off and tumbled to the ground whenever he moved.

"We were just in the wrong place at the wrong time," he said.

Julie gave him a sour smile.

"I know the feeling." She stood and pointed down at the gnome. "If anything happens to him, you'll hear from my lawyers."

"Okay, okay," Nick said, putting up his hands. So many mud clods broke free and fell to his feet, it looked like he was standing in the nastiest corner of an elephant cage. "You don't have to worry about me and my sister. We wouldn't go anywhere near any neighbor's property."

Before Julie could reply or even roll her eyes, Tesla came bursting out the back door. She was in a bathrobe, and her hair was still soaking wet.

"Nick, come here," she said. "I want to show you something."

She started marching across the lawn toward Mr. Jones's yard.

"But, Tez—" Nick said.

"Come on!"

Nick offered Julie an apologetic shrug—cracking off the mud-crust from his shoulders in the process—then turned to hustle away after his sister.

Tesla didn't stop until she was standing by the old but gleaming black Cadillac in Mr. Jones's driveway. She knelt beside one of the rear wheels.

"You ran out of the shower to show me a hubcap?" Nick said.

"No," Tesla said, pointing at the spotless hubcap anyway. "I ran out here because you were right all along and I didn't want to say it where someone might hear me."

Nick squatted and pretended to find the hubcap fascinating.

"Are you saying there is a spy in the house? How do you know?"

"I took off my pendant before getting in the shower," Tesla said. "When I got out, it was gone. Someone came into our room and stole it."

"Stole your pendant? But why?"

"I'd rather know *who*."

"Let's go find out, then," Nick said. He stood and put clenched fists on his hips. "The scientific way."

Shards of dried mud rained from his sides to form a crumbly pile on Mr. Jones's driveway.

"After I take a shower," Nick added.

FINGERPRINT-FINDER POWDER AND EVILDOER IDENTIFICATION SYSTEM

THE STUFF

- A fine emery board (also known as a nail file)

- A sharpened pencil

- An object you suspect might have fingerprints on it

- Gloves (optional)

- Clear tape

- An index card

THE SETUP

1. Hold the emery board and pencil over the object you're examining and lightly scratch the pencil lead with the emery board to create a fine powder on the object's surface. If anyone

   has touched it, the sweat and oil on their skin will have left impressions in the shape of the tiny (and completely unique) ridged pattern on their fingers. If you have to move the object, wear gloves to keep your own prints off it.

2. If you see a fingerprint, continue to scratch the pencil on the nail file until the print is fully revealed. Sometimes lightly blowing on the object helps spread the powder.

THE FINAL STEPS

1. To preserve the fingerprint as evidence, apply a piece of tape to the print and lift it off the object. Tape the print onto an index card and write down where you found it.

2. Analyze the fingerprint, looking for the three basic formations: arches, loops, and whorls.

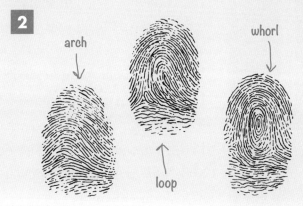

3. Gather fingerprints from your suspects. The clearest prints will be on smooth surfaces, like glass.

4. Compare the prints.

5. Catch the culprit!

"The pendant was right there, next to my clothes," Tesla said, pointing at the floor.

She and her brother were in their bedroom on the second floor of Uncle Newt's house. Both of them were wearing bathrobes now. (Nick had insisted on showering off his crunchy mud coating before he'd begin hunting for clues.)

At their bare feet were a muck-covered T-shirt and jeans.

"Geez, Tez," Nick groused. "You are such a slob sometimes."

"I was in a hurry to get all that gunk off me, okay? Anyway, we're not here to critique my housekeeping skills. We're here to find a fingerprint. So let's get to it."

"Right."

Both Nick and Tesla were holding nail files and pencils, and they crouched down and began rubbing them together.

"It's a good thing Uncle Newt doesn't have shag carpet," Nick said. "This hardwood floor should be perfect for—hey! I think I already got one!"

Tesla peered over at the fine black filings of pencil lead on the floor in front of her brother.

He was right. A pattern was emerging.

Nick leaned in and blew lightly on the powder. As it spread, another pattern appeared. Then another. Then another and another.

They hadn't just found a single fingerprint. They'd found five!

Tesla helped Nick cover them with more powder. After a bit more careful blowing, though, it became clear that four of the prints were smudged.

"I think the thief's fingers only brushed over the floorboards when he or she picked up your pendant," Nick said. "The middle finger's always the longest, though. It looks like it pressed down a little harder than the others. See?"

Indeed, the middle print was clearer than the rest and had the oval shape Tesla expected from fingerprints. The others were more like smears. Useless.

"Give me the tape," Nick said. "I'm gonna try to lift the print."

Tesla pulled a roll of Scotch tape from the pocket of her bathrobe and handed it to her brother.

"Be careful," she said.

Nick glowered at her—when was he *not* careful?—then broke off a piece of tape about two inches long. Slowly, carefully, he brought it down toward the little black ridges and swirls on the floor. He pressed the tape onto them and waited a moment. Then he lifted.

The fingerprint came up with the tape.

"It worked," Nick said. "*It actually worked!*"

"You say that like you're surprised," Tesla said.

"I am," Nick admitted. "I got that trick from a movie."

While Nick beamed proudly at the tape, Tesla pulled an index card and marker from the other pocket of her bathrobe.

"Well, you can't just sit there staring at it all day," she said.

She put the card on the floor in front of her brother.

He nodded, stuck the tape to the card, and then picked up the marker.

On the back of the card he wrote **THE BAD GUY (OR LADY)**.

"Not necessarily," Tesla said when she read the words. "I just realized whose prints we have to compare that sample to first."

"Whose?"

Tesla cocked an eyebrow, held up her hands, and wiggled her fingers.

"Oh," Nick said. "Right."

It was their room. They had to make sure the fingerprint wasn't one of theirs.

If it was, they had nothing.

Nick and Tesla were hunched over three index cards. One had **THE BAD GUY (OR LADY)** written on it. One had **TESLA** written on it. One had **NICK** written on it.

The **TESLA** and **NICK** cards also had two black

smudges on them: the prints from each of their middle fingers. (Every finger has a different pattern on the skin, and because Nick and Tesla weren't sure if the print they'd picked up from the floor was from a right or left hand, they had to check both of their own.)

For several minutes, the kids moved their gazes from one card to the next to the next, then back to the first to start over.

"The print from your left is kind of loopy," Tesla said. "But the print from your right is kind of archy."

"Your left is kind of whorly," said Nick. "But your right is kind of swirly." He squinted even harder at the black pattern. "And I think I see a clown in it."

Tesla rolled her eyes. "Knock it off. We're not staring at clouds."

They went back to examining the cards in silence.

"Who knew CSI work was so boring?" Nick said eventually.

"Not me," said Tesla.

Another minute went by.

"I don't see anything that matches," Tesla announced.

"Me neither," said Nick. He smiled and tapped

the **BAD GUY** card. "So this is from the spy."

Tesla shook her head.

Nick's grin wilted.

"Who else could it be from?" he said.

"Uhh, maybe *the guy who owns this house*."

"Oh. Right. Uncle Newt."

Tesla nodded. "We need to make sure that print's not from him. Which means we have to fingerprint him without tipping off the spy."

Nick's smile returned.

"No, we won't," he said. "I know where Uncle Newt's already left us all the fingerprints we'll need."

Nick and Tesla got dressed, went downstairs to the kitchen (passing the maids, who were debating whether to vacuum the polar bear in the hallway), and found a jumbo bag of spicy pork rinds in the pantry. They smuggled it back upstairs under Nick's T-shirt.

No one in the house touched pork rinds except Uncle Newt. Ever. No matter how many times he said, "Oh, come on, kids—it's just like potato chips made out of deep-fried pig skin. Doesn't that sound delicious?"

Nick and Tesla didn't even have to bother dusting the bag for prints. It was covered with them already. They were bright red—the same color as the fiery seasoning coating the rinds.

After a few minutes looking from the BAD GUY card to the bag and back again, Nick and Tesla turned to each other.

"Not him," said Tesla.

"Not him," said Nick. "Which means we really, truly, this-time-for-sure *know* that the fingerprint on the floor came from the spy."

"Yes."

"Excellent! Finally! Progress! Now all we have to do is get samples from all of our suspects and . . . then . . ."

A haunted, hopeless look came over Nick's face as his words trailed off.

"You haven't thought about *how* we're going to get all those sample fingerprints, have you?" Tesla asked him.

Nick shook his head forlornly.

Tesla put a hand on his shoulder.

"That's okay," she said. "Because I have."

"Time for lemonade!" Tesla said with a smile.

She stepped into the living room balancing two glasses on a silver serving tray.

The maids peered up at her. They were in the middle of the room fighting to pull a wad of dust and hair as big as a basketball from their clogged-up vacuum cleaner. Other than a single strip along the floor that seemed slightly less filthy than the floor around it, the room didn't look any different than it had when the maids showed up that morning. Dust-covered books and cables and beakers and rotting bananas were still piled everywhere.

At the maids' rate of progress, they might have the house clean in time for Christmas. Maybe.

"No, thanks," said the maid with a mole on her nose.

"Maybe later," said the maid with a mole on her chin.

They were both teeny, wrinkled women with white, poofy permed hair and black-rimmed cat's-eye glasses. The moles were the only way Tesla could tell them apart.

"Are you sure?" Tesla said, giving the tray a little shake so the ice in the lemonade tinkled enticingly. "Homemade."

This was *kind of* true. Tesla had poured the powdered drink mix into the pitcher and added water right there in the kitchen of Uncle Newt's home.

"That's awful nice of you, but we have a lot to do right now," said Chin Mole.

"We'll let you know when we're ready for a break," said Nose Mole.

They went back to tugging on the dust bunny, which was, unlike other dust bunnies, the size of an actual (and extremely well-fed) rabbit.

"How could there be so much hair in there already?" Nose Mole grumbled. "The darned cat's *bald.*"

The maids glanced back over their shoulders.

Tesla was still standing there with the tray in her hands.

"I'm Tesla, by the way," she said.

"I'm Ethel," said Chin Mole.

"I'm Gladys," said Nose Mole.

"We're busy," said Chin Mole.

Tesla widened her smile and gave her eyes a glassy, oblivious glaze she'd learned from Uncle Newt.

"Oh, I bet!" she said. "I'm sorry we've made so much work for you around here."

"No need to apologize," said Ethel (not adding, but plainly thinking, "No need for you to talk at all.").

"It's what we get paid for," said Gladys.

She didn't look happy about it.

"Of course. I understand," said Tesla. "Could you do me a favor while you're doing your thing?"

Gladys and Ethel put on identical dubious expressions.

"Maybe," Gladys said warily.

"Could you keep your eyes out for a silver necklace with a star-shaped pendant?" Tesla said. "I lost it, and it means a lot to me. I'd do anything to get it back."

"When did you lose it?" Ethel asked.

"Today."

Ethel and Gladys pinched their lips and narrowed their eyes.

"Oh, I'm not accusing anyone!" Tesla said. "I'm sure it was my fault. I was in such a hurry to get in the shower. You saw how dirty I was when I came in a little while ago."

"Oh, yeah," said Ethel.

"We sure did," said Gladys.

Their steely gazes flicked, for just a second, to the trail of dirt clods that ran along the hall and up the stairs.

"I'm so mad at myself I could just scream," Tesla said. "That necklace was a gift from my parents, you see, and my brother and I haven't seen them in weeks. They went off to Uzbekistan for some kind of work thing, and now we don't know when—or if—we'll see them again."

Tesla did her best to work up a tear.

When she thought about her mom and dad, it wasn't all that hard.

"Anyway," she said, sniffling and putting on what she hoped would look like a brave but tremulous smile. "You're sure you won't have some lemonade? I juiced two dozen lemons to make it."

"Well . . ." Ethel said.

"Oh, go on," said Tesla. "I absolutely refuse to leave till you've tried it."

That did the trick.

Ethel walked over, took a glass, and chugged down every drop.

Gladys stepped up beside her, grabbed the other glass, and took a single sip.

"Yum," she grunted.

She slammed the glass down and went back to the vacuum cleaner.

Ethel wiped her mouth with the back of her wrinkled hand, returned her own glass to the tray, then joined her partner.

"Just let me know if you want more!" Tesla said.

"We'll do that," Gladys said.

She and Ethel turned their little, hunched backs to Tesla and began yanking on the hair ball again.

A moment later, Tesla was sliding the serving tray onto the counter in the kitchen. A marker was waiting for her there, and she picked it up and wrote a single, small letter on each glass.

G for Gladys.

E for Ethel.

She didn't need powder to see that both glasses were covered with fingerprints.

"Time for lemonade!" Nick said with a smile.

He was coming down the stairs to the basement laboratory holding two glasses perched precariously on a plate. (Tesla had bought the right to use the serving tray for one million dollars.)

Uncle Newt and Oli looked up from their work. Uncle Newt was on one side of the lab trying to set an apricot on fire with a Bunsen burner. Oli was on the other side of the lab scrubbing black banana goo out of a scorched engine block. Neither looked very pleased with his progress.

"Lemonade!" said Uncle Newt.

"Le Monade?" said Oli.

Uncle Newt hopped to his feet and began winding his way past the clutter-covered worktables and discarded experiments and humming, clanking, sometimes sizzling and smoking machines that filled the lab.

Oli just stared dubiously at the glasses on Nick's plate. He wasn't wearing his fedora and trench coat any longer, but he didn't look much more comfortable: now he was in a tight black suit with a thin black tie. He was wearing sunglasses, too, even though the lab was lit by only a few flickering fluorescent tubes in the ceiling.

"Don't you have lemonade in Australia?" Nick asked him.

"Oh, of course," Oli said. "But . . . uhh . . . I did not recognize it. In Australia, it is . . . you know . . ."

Oli grimaced and rolled his hands in the air.

Nick waited patiently for him to finish his thought.

"Different," Oli finally said.

"Well, come try some American-style," Nick said.

"Yes," Oli said, still grimacing. "I am most excited to."

He started toward Nick with all the speed and eagerness of a man walking the plank. He'd barely taken three steps in the time it took Uncle Newt to reach Nick.

"Thanks," Uncle Newt said, snatching one of the glasses. "This'll really hit the spot. Who knew burning fruit could make a man so thirsty?"

He gulped down half of his lemonade, then smacked his lips.

"Delightful!" he declared. "Hmm . . . I wonder if lemons are flammable."

"See?" Nick said to a still doubtful-looking Oli. "It's good. And good for you. Fresh-squeezed juice, full of vitamin C. You know. Kind of like jelly."

Oli stepped up, took a deep breath, and then reached toward the plate.

Got ya, Nick thought as the man's big, thick fingers wrapped around the remaining glass.

Oli lifted it, sniffed the contents, and took a tiny sip.

His lips puckered, then slowly spread into a smile.

"Oh. *Lemon*ate. Yes!" He took another sip. "Is good! Just like back in Australia. I will enjoy more as I work."

He turned and headed back to the engine he'd been cleaning—taking the glass with him.

"Where'd you get the lemons?" Uncle Newt said.

Nick had to tear his gaze away from the glass—and the fingerprints—that were moving away from him.

"Huh?"

"The lemons. For the lemonade," Uncle Newt said. "Where are they from? I sure didn't buy 'em. You know how I feel about fruit. If I'm not gonna let it rot and use it for fuel, I don't want anything to do with it!"

"Oh. Well. Umm. Tez and I got the lemons from . . . Mr. Jones's lemon tree."

Nick was too busy worrying about getting Oli's glass back to come up with a good lie.

Mr. Jones didn't have a lemon tree.

Fortunately, Uncle Newt probably wouldn't have noticed a giant beanstalk growing in his neighbor's yard.

"Oh, sure, of course," he said. He took another big gulp. "Funny . . . all that extra effort, and it still tastes like the powdered stuff."

There was a sudden clatter and crash from the other side of the lab, and Oli cried out a word Nick didn't recognize (though he got the distinct impression it *wasn't* English and it *was* extremely impolite).

Oli had bumped into one of Uncle Newt's discarded experiments—a solar-powered pogo stick for dogs that was supposed to "change the face of fetch forever"—and dropped his lemonade.

"I mean, darn," Oli said, looking down at the shards of glass at his feet.

That's what you get for wearing sunglasses in a basement, Nick could've said to him. But he was too grateful for his lucky break to gloat.

"Don't worry! I'll take care of it!" he said, hurrying to get the broom he knew was gathering cobwebs in a corner.

Soon he had what was left of the drinking glass swept up onto the plate he'd been using as a tray.

"I am sorry," Oli said. "I was enjoying the lemon . . . uh . . . drink."

"I'll bring you more," Nick said as he started toward the stairs. "When I have time to squeeze more lemons."

He went up a few steps, then stopped.

"Oh, by the way—have either of you seen a silver necklace? With a star-shaped pendant on it? Tesla lost it this morning."

Uncle Newt shook his head.

"We've been down here all morning—right, Oli? Well, except for when I sent you up to get me more banana pulp."

Oli nodded grimly at the memory.

"Yes," he said. "But I did not see necklace or pendant. Just rotten bananas. And gnats."

He pronounced the last word "guh-nats."

Nick was pretty sure even people from Australia would say "nats."

"All right. I'm sure she just left it somewhere. Thought I'd check, though," he said. "Later!"

"What will be later?" Nick heard Oli ask Uncle Newt as he headed up the stairs.

When he got to the kitchen, he carefully inspected the biggest piece of glass on the plate. It was covered with greasy brown-black smudges. The fingerprints of a man who'd spent his morning working with banana pulp—and perhaps sneaking away to do more.

"Time for lemonade!" Tesla said with a smile.

She was climbing the ladder that led to the attic, a single glass in her hand. (Bringing it on the serving tray would have been classier, but Tesla figured she'd have dropped it halfway up.)

Skip the Verminator exterminator turned to look at her as she popped up into the cramped, cluttered attic. There were cobwebs everywhere—in corners, on rafters, on shelves and trunks and boxes—and he was poking at one with the end of his spray nozzle.

"Lemonade?" he said. He turned back to the cobweb and spritzed it with pesticide. "Can't stand the stuff."

Tesla finished climbing up into the attic. The air was musty and stiflingly hot.

"Maybe just a nice, cool glass of water, then?" she said. "You've gotta be thirsty."

"Nope. I hydrated thoroughly before coming up here." Skip leaned in close to the web he'd just sprayed and then nodded with brusque satisfaction. "I'm a professional, kid."

He turned and walked straight into another spider web.

"Eww! Ahh! Eee!" Skip squealed, dancing in a circle and slapping frantically at himself. "Is it on me? Is it on me?"

Before Tesla could answer, he began squirting his jumpsuit with bug spray.

This did not strike Tesla as standard operating procedure for a professional.

Something the size and color of a corn flake dropped off the man's chest and began scurrying away.

Skip stomped on it so hard Tesla was surprised his heavy work boot didn't smash through the floorboards and poke out the kitchen ceiling.

Slowly, warily, the panting exterminator lifted his boot and peeked at what was underneath.

"Yup. That was a black widow, all right," he announced, even though the spider he'd stepped on was now little more than a tiny brown stain on the attic floor. "Good thing I'm here."

He wiped a dangling wad of stray spider web from his mustache and then turned and moved deeper into the shadows.

"Thanks for the waitressing, kid," he said without looking back at Tesla. "But I've got serious work to do, and it'll be better for everyone if I'm not distracted."

"Sure. Sorry. I understand," Tesla said. "But before I go . . ."

She scanned the attic, searching for the perfect prop.

The ray-gun-looking thing on the shelf? Too close.

The night vision goggles on the plastic Santa? Too far.

The jet pack in the corner? Too big.

The boxes labeled BIOHAZARD and PROPERTY OF U.S. GOVERNMENT and DANGER: IRRADIATED? Too freaky.

The huge, misshapen, web-covered skull? Waaaaaaay too freaky.

The equally huge, equally misshapen, equally web-covered plaster outline of a foot? Equally freaky—but it would have to do.

"Could you bring that to me?" Tesla said.

When Skip turned to look at her, she pointed at the foot. It was on a shelf near the room's one dingy, dust-fogged window.

"What do you need *that* for?" Skip said with surprise and, it seemed to Tesla, a trace of distrust.

Perhaps he suspected—correctly—that he was being conned somehow.

"It's for a project I'm working on, but I've been too scared to come up and get it," Tesla told him. "You know—because of the black widows. But as long as a professional's here . . ."

Skip eyed the foot uneasily.

"No problem," he croaked.

He cleared his throat, started toward the foot, and then stopped.

"What's the project?" he asked.

"It's for my cryptozoology club. That's a casting of a genuine *Fakeulus teslapithicus* footprint. I'm going to do a side-by-side comparison with the toe splay of your standard *Imaginarium bogusapien*."

"Oh, okay," Skip said, sounding as though he hadn't understood a word of Tesla's answer.

Which was appropriate, since it wasn't supposed to make sense anyway. It was supposed to make someone say "Oh, okay" and immediately drop the subject.

And it worked. Skip didn't say another word as he crept toward the footprint. When he reached it, he used his spray nozzle to pull off as many cobwebs as he could. Then he gave it a squirt here, a squirt there, even a squirt between each toe.

When he was satisfied that nothing was going to crawl out and bite him, he pinched one of the toes with the index finger and thumb of his left hand, lifted, and whipped around toward Tesla.

"Here—take it take it take it take it!" he said as he scuttled toward her.

He wasn't touching the foot with his middle finger at all. Tesla wouldn't be getting the one fingerprint she really needed.

She officially ran out of patience.

"*Hey*," she snapped at Skip just as he reached her with the foot. "*Just hold this, would you?*"

She thrust the glass of lemonade at him.

Skip handed her the foot and took the glass, looking confused.

"Thanks," Tesla said.

She lifted the plaster footprint over her head, pretended to inspect the bottom for . . . well, something, and then nodded in fake satisfaction.

"Perfect," Tesla said, tucking the foot under her arm. "Thanks."

She reached out and took the glass, careful to cradle it from underneath rather than wrap her hand around it.

"I'll leave you to your work now," she said. But just as she started easing down the steps, she paused. "Oh, one last thing. I lost a necklace this morning. Silver with a star-shaped pendant. Have you seen it?"

"Oh, that?" Skip said. "Sure. I've got it right here."

Tesla's eyes went wide as the exterminator stuffed a hand into a jumpsuit pocket.

Was getting the pendant back going to be this easy? Was its disappearance just some kind of misunderstanding? Was there really a spy in the house at all?

Skip pulled his hand out of his pocket, held it out toward Tesla, and opened it wide, revealing . . . nothing.

"Oops. My bad. I *don't* have your necklace," Skip said. "*Because I'm not a thief.*"

Tesla stifled a groan.

"I'm sorry. I didn't mean to accuse you of anything," she said. "I probably just dropped it and I was hoping maybe—"

"Whatever, kid," Skip cut in. "Do you think you could let me do my job now?"

"Right. Sorry. I'll just go and . . ." Tesla squinted at Skip's right shoulder. "Whoa. Is that thing *moving*?"

"What? Ugh! Bleah!" the exterminator cried, beating himself with a flattened hand. "Did I get it? Did I get it? Did I get it?"

Tesla peered at Skip's shoulder again.

"You know what?" she said. "I think it was just some dandruff. Good luck with the spiders!"

Tesla went down the ladder as quickly as she could.

Nick was sitting on the floor hunched over an index card when Tesla came into their bedroom and shut the door behind her.

"Do you think Oli spells his name O-L-I or O-L-Y?" Nick asked, tapping the end of a pen against his chin.

He looked up at his sister and dropped the pen.

"What the heck is that?" he asked, staring in dismay at the massive plaster foot under Tesla's arm.

"A footprint. Duh," Tesla said.

She dropped it on her bed and knelt down next to Nick.

"I know it's a footprint. But from what?" he said. "A Wookiee?"

"One mystery at a time," Tesla said.

She picked up the emery board and pencil on the floor beside her brother and got to work on the glass she'd just brought down from the attic.

A few minutes later, the kids had five index cards spread out in front of them, each with its own neatly written label.

ETHEL
GLADYS
UNCLE NEWT
OLI/OLY
VERMINATOR SKIP

"There. We're ready," Nick said. "Now we compare these to the thief's prints and find out who our spy is. Get the other card."

"Right."

Tesla stood and went to a nearby dresser. She and her brother had hidden the card with the culprit's fingerprint on it in one of the top drawers, under Nick's socks.

Tesla opened the drawer and slipped a hand inside.

Then she began sifting around in the socks.

Then she began tossing socks over her shoulder while saying, "Oh, no no no no no."

She yanked open the other drawers and sent T-shirts and swimsuits and underwear flying in all directions.

"No no no no no no *no!*"

"What is it?" Nick asked. "What's wrong?"

But he already knew the answer.

Tesla backed away from the dresser and drooped down onto her bed beside the big foot.

"We're idiots," she said.

Nick couldn't disagree.

The card with **THE BAD GUY (OR LADY)** written on it was gone.

"We got evidence on a thief and then left it in our room," Nick said.

He was slumped on his bed, across from Tesla and the plaster foot.

Tesla said nothing.

"Even though we knew the thief was still around," Nick said.

Tesla stared off at nothing.

"And we knew the thief had already been in our room once before," Nick said.

Tesla just kept staring.

"And we were going to be leaving the room empty while we went around gathering—"

"I already said we were idiots!" Tesla snapped. "You don't have to keep reminding me why!"

"I know. I'm sorry. It's just that I can't believe it."

A moment went by in silence.

"I mean . . . we just left it in our room," Nick said. "Even though the thief was still here. And he'd already been in our—"

"Stop it!"

Tesla sprang up from her bed and began pacing and turning, pacing and turning.

"So we lost our only evidence," she said. "That's a setback, yeah. But we have another chance. Like you say, we know the thief is still around. And we know what he or she wants—and we have another one just like it."

Tesla stopped pacing and whirled around to face her brother.

It took him a few seconds to understand what

she meant.

"This?" he said, pointing to a little lump under his shirt.

His pendant.

Tesla nodded.

"That'll be our bait. Only we won't try to track down the thief after he or she steals it," she said. "This time, we're going to catch the bad guy red-handed."

RING-A-DING-DING
SPY EXPOSURE SYSTEM

THE STUFF

- A bicycle bell

- 1 1.5–3 volt motor

- 1 AA battery

- Duct tape

- 2 dimes or small metal washers

- 2 popsicle sticks

- 1 rubber band

- Wire (22-gauge, single-strand wire works best)

- A plastic cap from a pen

- Aluminum foil

- A CD case

- Hot-glue gun

- Bait (whatever you think a thief would be after!)

1. Remove the lower part of the bicycle bell's handlebar mount and apply a good amount of hot glue to each tab where the screws had been.

2. Glue the bell onto one side of the CD case, making sure that the thumb ringer faces out. (If you don't have a CD case, just use some cardboard.)

3. Cut two wires as long as the distance you want the alarm to be from the trigger. Cut another wire about 3 inches (5 cm) long. Strip the plastic from about ¾ inch (2 cm) of each end of all three wires.

4. Twist one end of one of the long wires and one end of the short wire onto the metal tabs of the motor, taking care to ensure that they both make good contact with the tabs.

5. Carefully push out the tabs.

6. Cut two strips of duct tape about ½ inch (1 cm) wide.

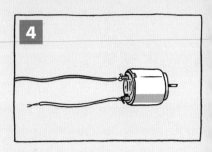

7. Arrange the dimes, one piece of duct tape, and the motor as shown. Make sure the motor is in the center and the dimes are equally spaced from it.

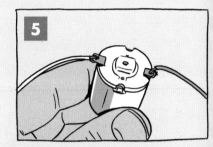

8. Place the second piece of duct tape across the other side of the dimes and press the tape to secure everything. The tape and dimes should be able to spin freely.

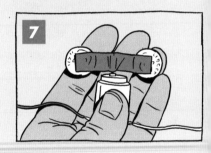

9. Put hot glue (not too much!) where each wire attaches to the motor and secure it all to the CD case so that the dimes touch the bicycle bell when they spin. Be sure to keep the glue away from the center shaft of the motor.

10. Tape the free end of the short wire to one end of the battery and the other long wire to the opposite end of the battery. Make sure they make a good connection.

11. Glue or tape the battery to the CD case, and the alarm's complete!

THE FINAL STEPS

1. For the trigger, fold the exposed end of one long wire over a popsicle stick and glue it in place as shown. Repeat with the other long wire and popsicle stick.

2. Wrap a small piece of aluminum foil around the end of each stick, making certain it touches the wire. This will help ensure that the sticks have good contact when the alarm is tripped.

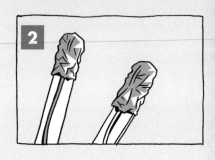

3. Loosely wrap the rubber band around the center of the popsicle sticks and place the pen cap between them as shown below. When the two wired ends of the sticks touch, the alarm sounds. That'll get old *real* fast, so while you're setting up the alarm you'll probably want to put a piece of paper between the sheets of foil.

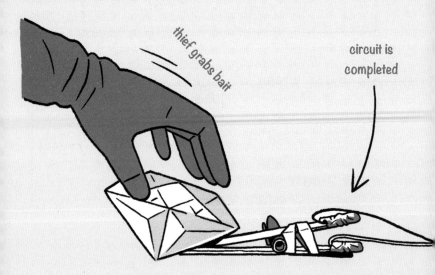

thief grabs bait

circuit is completed

4. Place the bait on the popsicle sticks so that the two active ends of the sticks separate. You might need to loosen the rubber band.

5. When the thief takes the bait, the wired ends of the popsicle sticks will touch, completing the circuit and activating the motor. The dimes will begin spinning—and the bell will begin ringing.

6. Hide nearby, listen for the alarm, and get ready to catch a thief!

alarm goes off!

usually worked on their experiments and gadgets in the basement. When you're wannabe inventors and you've got a real-life, honest-to-goodness laboratory in the house, you use it.

Except when a possible spy's there scrubbing scorched banana gunk out of an engine block, that is.

Oli the apprentice was still with Uncle Newt in the basement. So Tesla stayed there only long enough to gather what she needed for the alarm.

"I want to see if I can make a Barbie walk," she said when Uncle

Newt asked her why she needed a mini motor, duct tape, and wire.

(Tesla did have a Barbie doll, but at the time it was under a pile of dirty clothes in her bedroom on the other side of the country.)

She hurried upstairs, passing the maids, who were trying to figure out how to clean Spaghettios off the ceiling and how they got there in the first place. Then she and Nick got to work in their room.

A long, frustrating hour passed before Tesla's idea became a reality. Because Nick's necklace and pendant were so light, they wouldn't hold down the ends of the popsicle sticks (and keep the alarm from sounding prematurely) until the rubber band was loosened so much that it barely held the sticks together at all. But on the twentieth try, Tesla was able to wind the band around the sticks with precisely the right amount of tightness . . . or so it seemed. She couldn't be sure the whole thing wouldn't fall apart the second she and Nick turned their backs.

Nick apparently felt the same way.

"You know, with your pendant gone, mine's our last connection to Mom and Dad," he said. "If those things are tracking devices, that means Agent McIntyre won't be able to find us without them. We're risking a lot on a trap that might not work."

"I know that, Nick," Tesla said. "But what else are we gonna do? Just sit around waiting for Mom and Dad's enemies to come grab us?"

Nick thought it over and then sighed.

"Yeah. I'd probably have a nervous breakdown that way anyhow. We may as well do *something* while we await our doom."

"Geez . . . way to keep things positive, Little Mr. Sunshine," Tesla said. "Have some faith, would ya?"

It was then that the rubber band came loose, the plastic cap holding the popsicle sticks apart rolled free, and the whole trigger mechanism collapsed.

"You were saying . . . ?" Nick said to Tesla.

"No biggie. I'll just put the rubber band back on, and it'll be good as new. Only take a sec."

As Tesla worked, she didn't ask Nick if he'd changed his mind about her plan. She didn't want to give him the chance to say yes.

Rewinding the rubber band took more than a sec. It took a couple hundred. But eventually the alarm was ready again (Tesla hoped).

That didn't mean the trap was ready, though.

"We know there's someone in the house who'll steal a pendant," Nick said. "But how do we let him or her know there's another pendant to steal?"

Tesla was about to say the three words she hated most in the world—"I don't know"—when she was saved by a sound from downstairs.

The doorbell was ringing.

"Maybe it's a new suspect." Tesla said. "We've had so many show up today, why not another?"

Nick crossed his fingers as he followed his sister down the stairs.

"Please be Agent McIntyre, please be Agent McIntyre, please be Agent McIntyre . . ."

It wasn't Agent McIntyre. It was Silas and DeMarco.

"We came to apologize," Silas said. He elbowed DeMarco. "Didn't we?"

"I'm sorry I laughed when you got splashed with mud," DeMarco said. "And I shouldn't have doubted you about . . ."

He peered past Nick and Tesla.

Ethel and Gladys were standing on the dining room table scrubbing the ceiling while Oli, still in his black suit and sunglasses, skulked around gathering bananas. From upstairs, the distant, muffled voice of Skip the exterminator could be heard saying, "Ugh! Argh! Get off me! Yuck!"

". . . the you-know-whats," DeMarco whispered.

"Don't worry about it," Tesla said, extra loud. "In fact, you came by at exactly the right moment. Nick was just saying he wanted to try your water-mud-stunt ramp himself."

Nick was about to say "I *what?*" but Tesla silenced him with a glare.

"Really?" Silas said, completely missing the signal. "It's not easy, man. DeMarco fell off four times before he finally made it to the bottom. I thought he was gonna break his neck!"

"Sounds like fun . . . *right, Nick?*" Tesla said.

Nick gritted his teeth.

"Oh, yeah," he said. "Just the kind of thing I love."

"Well, let's go then! Last one with a fracture's a rotten egg!"

Tesla shoved Nick toward Silas and DeMarco,

then stepped out and closed the door behind them.

"What was that all about?" DeMarco asked.

"Someone stole my pendant this morning," Tesla said. "Now we want to give them the chance to steal Nick's."

"You do?" DeMarco said.

Tesla stepped off the front porch and headed toward the street.

"Come on. I'll explain on the way."

Silas and DeMarco followed looking extremely confused.

Nick followed looking extremely unhappy.

He'd already figured out his sister's plan.

If the spy liked stealing things when people were in the shower, well, Nick was going to have to take another shower. Which meant he was going to need a *reason* to take another shower.

The reason was waiting for him at the bottom of a slide in DeMarco's backyard.

Ten minutes later, the front door opened again, and something brown and gloppy and very, very grumpy stomped into the house.

"Sorry about the floor!" Nick called to Gladys and Ethel, who gawked at him from atop the dining room table. "I'll help clean it when I'm out of the shower!"

As he started up the stairs, runny mud squishing in his pants with every step, he thought, *This better work, Tesla. 'Cuz if it doesn't, I'm gonna kill you.*

Tesla came in the back door laughing.

"Ha ha! Hilarious!" she said.

DeMarco was behind her.

"Ho ho! Awesome!" he said.

Silas came inside last.

"Hee hee! I'm so glad I was there to see Nick try to go down the slide on a bike and fall into the mud and get so messy he had to come home and take off all his dirty things and immediately get in the shower!" he said.

Tesla glowered at him.

He gave her a grin and a big thumbs-up.

Before they'd gone inside, Tesla had warned him not to lay it on too thick.

Apparently, he thought he was being subtle.

"So who wants something to drink?" Tesla said.

She opened the refrigerator.

"Me!" said DeMarco.

"Me, too!" said Silas. "Say—why don't we take our cool, refreshing beverages outside to enjoy in the warm summer sun? That way we won't be in anyone's way!"

Tesla made a mental note: Next time (if there ever was a "next time" for trying to catch a spy), Silas wouldn't be allowed to talk at all.

She opened the refrigerator and pulled out a bottle of diet soda.

"Whoa!" she cried, simultaneously jumping back and throwing the bottle at the fridge.

"What's wrong?" said DeMarco.

"I don't remember this part of the plan," Silas whispered.

"That's because it's *not* part of the plan," Tesla hissed back at him. "Look."

She pointed at the refrigerator. Something was lurking behind the soda bottle.

Slowly, cautiously, Silas and DeMarco came closer to look at it.

"Creepy," Silas said.

"Cool," said DeMarco.

Lying on its back in a glass bowl was a small black spider. On its abdomen was a red hourglass.

It was a black widow, one of the most poisonous spiders in the world. Right next to the ketchup.

"It's not moving," DeMarco said.

He kept getting closer.

Silas didn't.

"Maybe it's asleep," Silas said. "Or playing dead."

"It's not playing," Tesla said. "It's just dead."

"How do you know?" Silas asked.

"My uncle told me and Nick he found a black

widow and put it somewhere. We assumed he meant it was alive. But there's no lid on that bowl to keep the spider from getting out. It must have been dead when Uncle Newt found it. Even he wouldn't put a live black widow in the refrigerator in nothing but a bowl." Tesla rubbed her chin pensively. "I think."

DeMarco was so close to the refrigerator now, he was practically inside it.

"Ever seen one of these before?" he asked Tesla.

"Only pictures," she said, stepping up beside him.

"Same with me. It's hard to believe something that small could kill you."

DeMarco stretched a hand out toward the bowl.

"*Please* tell me you're not gonna touch it," Silas moaned.

"Why not? Tesla says it's dead."

"Oh, well, if someone thinks it might be dead, then why not? There's nothing gross or scary about touching dead things, right? Especially crazy-poisonous dead things. So, sure—help yourself. See what it tastes like while you're at it."

DeMarco threw a scowl at his friend.

"You're taking all the fun out of this, you know."

When he turned around again, the spider was an

inch from his face.

Tesla had taken the bowl out of the refrigerator and was gently pushing one of it's hairy legs.

The other side of the spider's body lifted up like a teeter-totter when Tesla pressed down on the leg.

The little corpse was totally stiff.

"You know, you're right, Silas," DeMarco said, taking a step back. "This is gross and scary."

Tesla walked the bowl over to the sink and turned on the tap.

"You don't have to drown it, Tez. It's dead, re-member?" Silas said. He scuttled back so far he ended up pressed against the wall. "Right?"

"I'm not drowning it. I'm conducting an experiment."

She filled the little bowl with water, then brought it back to the refrigerator.

"Yup," DeMarco said, stealing another peek at the spider as Tesla went past. "They float, all right."

"That's not the experiment." Tesla put the bowl back where she'd found it and closed the fridge door. "All right, guys—let's go outside."

"Right!" Silas said. "I've got an idea! Let's play a loud, lively game that will keep us distracted while

Nick finishes his shower!"

He gave Tesla another thumbs-up before heading out the back door.

Tesla changed her mind about trying to keep him quiet next time. If there ever *was* a next time, she'd just make him go home.

"Whee ha ha hee!" Silas said. "Tag is so much fun!"

He was standing on the back porch beside Tesla and DeMarco.

"Nobody in the house can hear you, Silas," DeMarco said.

"So . . . I should be louder?"

"No," Tesla said.

There was a thunking noise off to the right, and the kids turned to find Uncle Newt's neighbor Julie Casserly pounding a stake into the ground next to her new garden gnome. Taped to the stake was a sign:

PRIVATE PROPERTY
TRESPASSERS WILL BE PROSECUTED

When she looked up and noticed Tesla and her friends watching, Julie dropped her hammer and adjusted the sign so that it was pointed straight at them.

"Why is she so afraid someone's going to touch her elf?" Silas said.

"It's a gnome," Tesla corrected. "And she's not worried someone's gonna touch it. She's worried someone's gonna blow it up."

"She only moved in, like, a month ago," DeMarco said. "If she didn't want to live next to a mad scientist, she should've picked a different neighborhood."

Tesla was about to say "Good point" when she noticed Silas sticking a finger in his ear, a puzzled look on his face.

"Something wrong?" she asked him.

Silas wiggled the finger as if he were trying to scratch the side of his brain.

"There's a ringing in my ear," he said.

Then Tesla finally heard it, too.

"The alarm!"

She bolted toward the back door, with DeMarco right behind her.

"That's the alarm?" Silas said as he lumbered after his friends. "I was expecting more of a 'whoop whoop.'"

Tesla was already sprinting through the kitchen. When she burst through the door into the dining room, she found the maids there still scraping Spaghettios off the ceiling.

So Gladys and Ethel weren't the spies. That left Skip the exterminator and Oli the apprentice.

Tesla dashed up the hall, whipped herself around the banister, and began leaping up the staircase three steps at a time.

From up ahead, she could still hear the *ting-a-ling-a-ling* of the bicycle bell. And she heard footsteps, too.

The spy was coming to the top of the stairs.

It was confrontation time.

"Get ready!" Tesla said to DeMarco and Silas behind her.

Whichever was the spy, Skip or Oli, he'd have to barrel through all three of them to get downstairs to the door. Surely one of them could keep him from escaping—somehow.

Tesla was nine steps from the second floor now.

Then six.

Then three.

Then—

Uncle Newt appeared at the top of the stairs.

"Oh, there you are, Tesla," he said. "Look what I found!"

He was holding Nick's necklace and pendant.

Tesla stopped in her tracks, and DeMarco and Silas crashed into her back.

"I don't get it," Silas panted when he saw who had the pendant. "So your uncle's the—?"

"The sweetest man on Earth for looking for my pendant?" Tesla cut in. "Yes. Yes, he is."

A few yards beyond Uncle Newt, a head poked down beside the ladder to the attic.

Skip was leaning down to look at them.

Out of the corner of her eye, Tesla could see Ethel and Gladys moving into the hallway below to watch as well. Oli joined them, a phone in his hand.

"What is making ringing?" he said. "I try answering telephone, but only hear the nothing."

"Oh, that's just the timer on my Easy-Bake oven," Tesla said. "We're making a cake. I'd better go take it out before it burns."

She started up the last few steps as Oli scratched his head and said, "You make cake upstairs?"

Tesla squeezed past her uncle and hurried into her room. Once she had disconnected the alarm bell, she came back into the hall.

"I thought I melted the Easy-Bake oven when I was testing my heat-resistant aerosol cans," Uncle Newt said. "Which weren't heat resistant."

"Nick and I built a new one," Tesla said.

"Funny I didn't see it when I went into your—"

"Thanks for this," Tesla said, yanking the pendant

from her uncle's hands. "I think it's Nick's, though."

"How can you tell?"

Tesla ran her fingers over the chain, then held them up and waggled them.

The tips were brown and moist.

"Mud's still wet," Tesla said. "I lost my pendant hours ago. It'd be dry by now."

Uncle Newt applauded. "Very nicely reasoned! And I guess it wouldn't make sense if yours was so easy to find. I was going to my room for a fresh T-shirt—this one's starting to smell like burned apricots, bleah—when I happened to glance over and notice that pendant lying there practically screaming, 'I'm right here! Come get me!'"

Tesla forced out an unconvincing chuckle as she stole glances over at the ladder to the attic and down at the hallway below.

She and her uncle weren't being watched anymore, except by Silas and DeMarco. Skip, Ethel, Gladys, and Oli had all gone back to whatever they were doing before.

Which, in one case, was plotting against Tesla and Nick.

The spy trap had failed.

Nick walked out of the bathroom drying his hair with a towel. He froze when he noticed Tesla and Uncle Newt and Silas and DeMarco.

"What'd I miss?" he said.

The kids went to a spy-free zone—DeMarco's backyard—to plot their next move.

"We need a new trap," Nick said as everyone gathered around their temporary HQ—the sandbox. "Something more subtle. If it had been Oli or that exterminator guy or one of the maids with the pendant, they could have said the same thing as Uncle Newt: 'Oh, look what I found for you.'"

Tesla nodded in agreement. "We have to let them think they got away with it. At least for a while, so they can't lie their way out of it when we confront them."

"Them?" DeMarco said. "You think there's more than one spy?"

"No," said Tesla. "I just get tired of saying stuff like, 'I hope he or she messes up so we can catch him or her before he or she puts his or her real plan into action.'"

"Hey! I know how to catch him-her!" Silas announced.

He snatched a twig off the ground and began drawing in the sandbox.

This is what he was trying to sketch out:

"You wanted subtle," Silas said as he worked. "Well, how's this for subtle?"

Unfortunately, it's really, really hard to draw in sand, and Silas's blueprint ended up looking like this:

"Yeah, that's subtle, all right," DeMarco said. "So subtle I don't understand it at all."

Nick pointed at the blob in the upper left-hand corner.

"Is that a flying piano?"

"No!" Silas said. "It's the eagle that'll swoop down to catch the mouse after the he-she thief takes the pendant and pulls the string that lifts the box. We'll see the eagle and come catch her-him before she-he can escape."

"Huh?" said Nick.

"I still don't understand it," said DeMarco.

"Oh, come on, guys! Mouse, box, string, eagle! It's not that complicated!"

Silas began retracing everything in his diagram, trying to dig deeper with the stick. But the sand kept shifting, and everything looked like squiggles.

"What's that?" said Tesla.

DeMarco squinted at Silas's sand drawings.

"What's any of it?" he said.

"Not down there," Tesla said, her voice dropping low. "Behind us. In the woods. I heard something."

Silas started to turn around.

Tesla stopped him with a hand on his arm.

NICK AND TESLA'S SECRET AGENT GADGET BATTLE

"Don't move," she whispered. "Just listen."

For a long moment, the kids stood there by the sandbox, frozen. The only thing they heard were birds chirping and the occasional car driving by on the street and, after a while, the *pop-pop-pop* of Silas cracking his knuckles. (There was also a single "Oof" when DeMarco elbowed him to make him stop.)

But finally there it was: a rustling in the woods just beyond DeMarco's yard. Then a soft murmuring and a clear, distinct *click*.

"All right," Tesla whispered. "On the count of three we're gonna turn around and get 'em."

"Don't you mean, 'On the count of three we're gonna run for it'?" Nick said.

The only answer he got from his sister was "One . . . two . . . three!"

The kids spun and rushed toward the bushes and trees and brush.

"We know you're in there!" yelled Tesla.

"We've got you!" yelled DeMarco.

"You might as well give up!" yelled Silas.

"Ahhhhhhhh!" yelled Nick.

Two figures emerged from the shadows of the forest as the kids grew closer. They both struck defiant poses—feet spread wide, hands on hips, heads cocked.

"If you touch us, you're dead," said one.

"*Yeah*," said the other.

The kids stopped their charge.

"You!" DeMarco cried in horror.

The spies in the forest were his bitter, implacable foes.

His little sisters.

"What are you doing with *them*?" said the older of the two, seven-year-old Elesha. She pointed

at Nick and Tesla. "Mom and Dad told you they're troublemakers."

"*Yeah*," said little five-year-old Monique.

"This is none of your business," Silas told the girls.

Elesha scowled at him.

"Butt out, tubby," she said.

"*Yeah*," said Monique.

Silas opened his mouth to reply.

"No! Don't provoke them!" DeMarco said. A shiver shook his body. "You know what they're capable of."

Silas closed his mouth and took a big step back.

"Smart move, blubber-butt," said Elesha.

"*Yeah*," said Monique.

Silas's face reddened, but he didn't attempt a comeback.

"Why are you watching us?" DeMarco asked his sisters.

"Why do you think?" Elesha said. She held up a little yellow box in her right hand. "You're going down."

This time, Monique just smirked.

"What is that?" Silas asked.

"A disposable camera," Nick told him.

"The cheap, old-fashioned kind," said Tesla. "With film."

DeMarco sighed. "My mom and dad bought it for them when we were at Lake Tahoe for spring break. I knew they'd use it against me one day."

Elesha gave the disposable camera a little shake.

"We've got you playing with kids you're not supposed to, launching bottle rockets off the roof, and teepeeing Julie Casserly's trees," she said.

Silas turned to DeMarco.

"Teepeeing Julie Casserly's trees? That was you?" he said. "Without me?"

DeMarco gave him a sheepish shrug.

"All right," Tesla said to the girls. "What do you want for the camera?"

"What do you mean?" Elesha said.

"You wouldn't be standing here talking to us if you were going to go get DeMarco in trouble anyway. There's something you want."

Elesha whispered something to Monique.

"No deals!" Monique said.

Elesha whispered something else to Monique.

"No deals!" Monique said.

Elesha whispered to Monique again.

"No deals! No deals!" Monique said.

Elesha whispered to Monique one more time.

"Oh, okay," Monique muttered bitterly. "Deal."

They turned toward DeMarco.

"Your DS *and* all your games *and* five dollars *and* your allowance for the rest of the summer," said Elesha. "Or you're toast."

"Ouch," said Silas.

"Whoa," said Nick.

"Brutal," said Tesla.

"Deal," said DeMarco. He held out his hand. "Now give it to me."

"Sure," said Elesha.

She whipped the camera at him with all her might.

He managed to grab it out of the air two inches from his face.

"Don't worry about giving us the five dollars," Elesha said. "We already know where you hide your money." She gave the older kids a smile as sweet as sugar—mixed with rat poison. "Come on, Monique. Let's go play our new games."

"*Yeah.*"

Elesha and Monique linked arms and skipped off

singing "La la la la-la-laaaaaa."

"If only we could sic *them* on the spies," Nick said as the little girls pranced up the hill toward their house, still la-la-laaaaa-ing.

DeMarco shook his head. "We couldn't trust them to stay on our side."

He looked down at the boxy camera in his hands, then lifted it and pointed it at Silas.

"There's one shot left," he said, "so you may as well say, 'Cheese!'"

Silas opened his mouth but only got so far as "Ch—."

"Wait!" Tesla cried out, jumping in front of De-Marco.

"You want a group shot?" Silas said.

"No," Tesla said. "I want that camera."

DeMarco handed it to her.

"What for?" he asked.

But Nick already had it figured out.

"Ahhhh," he said. "Looks like we found our something more subtle."

SPY-BUSTING INVISICAM

THE STUFF

- A disposable camera

- 1 paper clip

- 1 12-inch (30-cm) piece of PVC pipe labeled "1 inch"

- 1 AA battery (can be a dead one)

- Fishing line

- An old picture frame at least 8 by 10 inches (20 by 25 cm)

- Pushpins

- Drill

- Hot-glue gun

- Clear tape

- Duct tape

- A picture you don't want from an old calendar or magazine

THE SETUP

1. Remove any backing from the picture frame. If the glass in the frame is loose, secure it with hot glue.

2. Place the camera at the bottom of the frame.

3. Measure from the shutter button on top of the camera to just below the top of the frame. Cut the PVC pipe to this length.

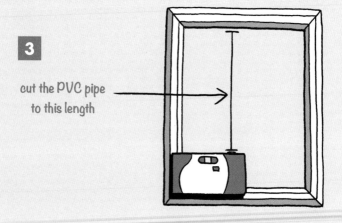

3

cut the PVC pipe
to this length

4. Once you've cut the pipe to the correct length, drill a ⅛-inch (0.3-cm) hole through both sides of the pipe 2¼ inches from the end.

5. Carefully center the other end of the pipe over the shutter button and use a couple dabs of hot glue to hold the pipe in place. (Don't get glue on the shutter button!) Make sure

the holes in the pipe are positioned to the sides of the camera.

6. Place the picture in the frame and cut a small hole where the camera lens will be.

7. Unbend the paper clip as shown and tie one end of the fishing line to the still-bent end of the paper clip. Slide the straight end of the clip through the holes in the pipe.

8. Insert the battery, with the positive (+) side down, into the top of the pipe.

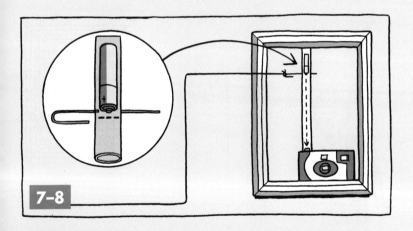

7-8

9. Secure the picture in the frame with clear tape.

10. Align the camera lens with the hole in the picture and use duct tape to hold the camera and pipe in place.

THE FINAL STEPS

1. Be sure you've wound the camera so that it's set to take a new picture.

2. Hang the camera at the best position and height to get a glimpse of the spy you're after. (Check with an adult before putting nails in the wall!) A flash will alert a spy that a picture's been taken, so pick a bright area where you won't need one.

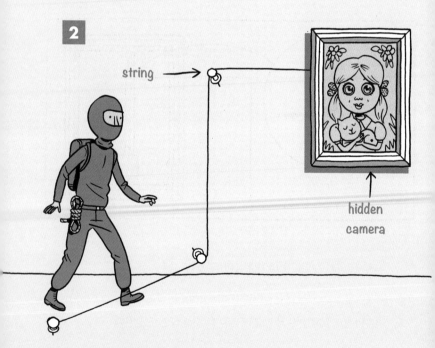

string →

hidden camera

3. Run the fishing line so that it will be pulled by an opening door, or string it across a doorway so that it will act as a trip wire. Lead the fishing line around pushpins or small wall hooks if it needs to curve around anything to reach the camera.

4. Leave the room.

5. On entering, the spy will pull on the fishing line by either opening the door or walking into the trip wire. The tug on the line will yank the paper clip from the pipe, allowing the battery to fall and hit the shutter button. *Click*.

6. Retrieve the camera and get the film developed. The last image on the roll will reveal the spy!

"Still trying to get Barbie to walk?" Uncle Newt asked when Nick and Tesla came to the lab to get supplies for the invisicam.

"Too easy," Tesla said. "Now we're trying to get her to dance."

"With G.I. Joe," said Nick.

"Who are these 'Barby' and 'Geeijo' who cannot do with the dancing?" Oli asked.

He was standing in a metal tub, trouser legs rolled up, feet buried in mounds of mashed brown bananas. (Uncle Newt had decided the bananas didn't have a high enough "muck factor" and made

Oli his designated squasher.)

"They're toys, Oli," Tesla said. "Don't you have those in Australia?"

"Only the . . . the . . ." Oli made a flicking movement with his hand. ". . . boomerung. Crikey. G'day!"

"That guy is not from Australia," Nick whispered to Tesla as they went up the stairs.

"I'm not sure he's from Earth," said Tesla.

When she and Nick reached the top of the stairs, they found Ethel and Gladys in the kitchen about to start cleaning the refrigerator.

"Oh, there's a black widow in there," Tesla said to them. "Don't throw it out, please."

The little white-haired maids shared a look.

"Let's do the sink instead," said Ethel.

"Right," said Gladys.

Nick and Tesla continued up to the second floor— where they found Skip the exterminator stepping out of their room.

"Well, you can rest easy tonight, kids," he said. "No spiders."

"What's that on your shoulder?" Nick asked.

Skip barked out a bitter laugh.

"What do you think I am, an idiot? I'm not falling

for that one twice!"

He turned and started toward Uncle Newt's room with the long, brown centipede still crawling up his shoulder, headed for his neck.

Nick and Tesla were in their room starting on the invisicam when they heard the scream.

Before Nick and Tesla came to stay with him, Uncle Newt had decorated their room with posters he assumed would appeal to kids. Most featured princesses, puppies, rainbows, or some combination of the three. (There was also a picture of Albert Einstein, but it had no princesses, puppies, or rainbows.)

Tesla picked out the poster she hated most—it showed a little girl with eyes the size of dinner plates saying "BUT I'M TOO CUTE TO DO HOMEWORK!"—and tore it down.

"Heh heh . . . I've been wanting to do this for weeks," she said as she started cutting the poster with a pair of scissors.

"Don't hack it up too much," Nick said. "Just enough to get it in the frame."

"I'll try to control myself."

When the poster was cut down to size, Nick and Tesla fitted it in the frame they'd sneaked off the wall downstairs. (Uncle Newt's patent for "Edible Cheese Jeans" was safely tucked away behind Tesla's bed so it could be returned to the frame later.) Once the picture was in place, the kids could see where the hole for the camera lens needed to be: right through the forehead of the puppy sitting at the lazy girl's feet.

"This just gets better and better," Tesla said with an evil grin.

"Cute" wasn't her thing.

Twenty minutes later, she and her brother were testing the fishing line they'd strung along the wall to the doorknob. When the door was opened, the pin was pulled from the PVC pipe duct-taped to the back of the picture frame.

The invisicam was going to work.

"Now we just need an excuse to leave your pendant lying around again," Tesla said.

"It'll have to be good," said Nick. "It'd be a pretty huge coincidence if I just happened to get dirty all over again some completely different way."

"Yeah . . . unless . . ."

Tesla got the same look in her eye that she'd had

while cutting a hole in the poster-puppy's head.

Nick's blood ran cold.

"What?" he said.

"What if it's not a coincidence at all," Tesla said, "because you went back for a second try at the thing you failed at before?"

"You mean . . . ? Oh, no! Again?"

Tesla nodded.

"Again."

"My mind's made up!" Nick boomed as he stomped down the stairs. "I know I can do it!"

Tesla rushed after him.

"But, Nick—you might end up more than muddy this time! You could get hurt!"

Nick caught a glimpse of Ethel and Gladys peeping out of the kitchen as he reached the bottom of the stairs. He pretended not to notice.

"Not gonna happen, Tez!" he said. "If DeMarco can jump a bike over that mud pit, so can I!"

He marched to the front door, Tesla still at his heels, begging him to stop.

As soon as they were outside with the door

closed behind them, Nick's forceful march turned into a reluctant trudge.

"I'm gonna get you for this," Nick grumbled.

"Fine," said Tesla. "So long as we get the spy first."

She hooked her arm around his and tugged him toward DeMarco's backyard.

Ten minutes later, Nick was back, looking like a giant Hershey bar that had been left out in the sun. He brought half the mud puddle with him. The only parts of him that weren't dripping brown muck were his eyes. They were throwing off sparks instead.

"Tesla lets her pendant get stolen, but *I'm* the one who pays for it," he muttered. "Next time, she can be the one to dive face-first into a mud puddle. Better yet, I'll throw her in."

He stopped on the porch, took a deep breath, then opened the door and stamped inside as loudly as he could.

"Sorry about the floor . . . again!" he shouted. "I'll clean it up when I'm out of the shower . . . again!"

He clomped through the hall and up the stairs. When he reached the second floor, though, his movements turned slow and smooth as he slipped into his room. He had to be careful not to open the door too wide and activate the invisicam.

The trap was set. All it needed now was bait.

Nick reached under his glop-soaked shirt and pulled out his pendant. It was the last gift his parents had given him. His only possible lifeline to Agent McIntyre. And, for the second time that day, he was about to leave it out to be stolen.

"See ya later," Nick whispered to it.

He dropped it on the floor.

"Or not."

Silas's backyard was more boring than DeMarco's. No sandbox, no swings, no slide, no mud pit. But there would be no Elesha and Monique skulking around, either. And no Mr. and Mrs. Davison (DeMarco's mom and dad) to call DeMarco inside because he and Silas were hanging around with one of those bad influences from up the street.

So Silas's yard was the logical rendezvous point. It had only that one downside.

"I'm bored," Silas said.

He was stretched out in the patchy grass gazing up at the sky. There were no clouds to look at, though. Above them was a big, solid ceiling of blue.

"Me, too," said DeMarco.

DeMarco wasn't the type to just lie down and stare up at nothing, so he was riding around the yard on his bike. The front wheel had developed a bad wobble after his third jump off the slide, and he was so bored he kept hoping it would fall off. He'd wipe out, sure, but at least that would be interesting.

"Just wait," Tesla told the boys. "You'll get some excitement soon enough."

Five minutes later, Nick showed up. He was wearing clean clothes (his third set of the day) and a dour expression.

"What's wrong?" DeMarco asked him. "Didn't your picture-trap-thing work?"

"The first part of it worked. Which is what's wrong," Nick said. "My pendant is gone. Someone stole it. As for the second part of the trap—"

He held up his right hand.

He was holding the disposable camera.

"I don't know if it worked or not . . . but this took a picture of *something*."

"Woo-hoo! We got him!" Silas exalted. "Now all we gotta do is plug the camera into a computer, and *pow*. There's the bad guy!"

He hustled across the sloping, weed-choked yard to give Nick a swat on the back.

"Cheer up, dude! You'll have your jewelry back by dinnertime!"

To Silas's surprise, Nick didn't look reassured.

"Plug the camera into a computer?" DeMarco said.

"Sure! Or just look on the little view-screen thingie on the back." Silas turned to Nick again and pointed at the camera in his hand. "Why haven't you checked it already?"

"Because it doesn't have a little view-screen thingie," Tesla said. "It's not a digital camera. It uses film."

"Oh, right. Old-school." Silas scratched his head. "So what do we plug it into?"

"You don't plug it into anything, Silas," Nick said. "You take the film to be developed."

Silas nodded.

"Got it!"

The nodding slowed.

"I think."

The nodding stopped.

"I don't get it."

"Come on," Tesla said, striding toward the street. "We'll show you."

Usually when the four friends rode their bicycles together, DeMarco would take the lead. He didn't want anyone in the way if there were potholes ahead, he always said. He didn't like to miss any.

This day, though, Nick ended up in front on the rusty old ten-speed his uncle had bought him at a garage sale. He knew where they had to go even if Tesla hadn't said it yet. DeMarco wasn't far behind him, but he had to work furiously just to keep up. His bike was still caked with mud from his jumps that morning, and the front wheel was wobbling and weaving wildly.

"Hey, DeMarco! I think you hurt your bike!" Tesla called out as they rode up the street toward the Pacific Coast Highway, the busy road that separated their neighborhood from downtown Half Moon Bay.

"Nah!" DeMarco shouted back to her. "The D-Rocket can take anything!"

"The D-Rocket" was DeMarco's bike.

The second it was on the other side of the highway, the front tire blew, the handlebar broke off, and the chain came loose, all in the span of half a second.

DeMarco let out a startled yip as the D-Rocket simultaneously swerved to the right and fell apart.

He made a much louder sound—a full-on "AHHHHHH!"—as Tesla, unable to steer away in time, slammed into him from behind.

Bicycles and riders hit the pavement in a tangled heap.

Nick and Silas skidded to a stop and hopped off

their bikes.

"Are you guys all right?" Nick said as he ran to Tesla and DeMarco.

"I'm okay," Tesla said. She looked down at De-Marco, who was pinned between her and the wreckage of the D-Rocket. "How about you?"

"I'll be better . . . when you're not . . . lying on me," DeMarco wheezed. "I think there's . . . a pedal . . . poking me somewhere . . . *really* sensitive."

"Oh! Sorry!"

Nick helped his sister get up.

Silas pulled DeMarco to his feet.

"Wow," said Nick. "Your bike is totaled, DeMarco."

"It's been worse," DeMarco said dismissively.

Nick didn't see how that could be true unless it had once been run over by a steamroller.

"How about your bike, Tez?" DeMarco said. "I hope it didn't get banged up too bad. It might not be as tough as the D-Rocket."

Tesla shot DeMarco a dubious look, then began separating the remnants of his bike from hers. The boys bent down to help. Soon, both bikes were on the sidewalk, one in pieces, one intact.

Tesla had appropriated her uncle's mountain

bike for the summer, and the only part that had come loose was a small, black metal square attached to the underside of the seat. It was hanging by a single corner now, and when Tesla started to push it back into place, she discovered that it was held in position with putty.

Tesla pulled instead of pushed on the black square, and it came free easily.

"What's that?" DeMarco asked.

"I have no idea."

Tesla held out the black square so everyone could get a look. It was about two inches across and half an inch thick, with a series of small holes on one side.

"Doesn't look like it would *do* anything," Nick said. "Unless there's something inside."

He and Tesla exchanged a somber look.

"What could be inside it?" Silas said. "That thing's barely big enough to hold a couple Cheerios."

"First things first," said Tesla, slipping the metal square into her pocket. "We need to get that picture developed. DeMarco, what do you want to do about your bike?"

DeMarco looked around. They were on the

edge of Half Moon Bay's downtown, just a couple blocks from Main Street, and not far away was a Dumpster-lined alley.

"I can leave the D-Rocket there for now," DeMarco said, nodding at the alleyway. He picked up the dented handlebar lying at his feet. "It's not like someone's going to ride off on it. And I'm guessing where we're going is right around the corner anyway."

"You're guessing right," Tesla said.

"How come everybody knows where we're going but me?" Silas said.

His friends chose not to answer.

The door chime rang, and Lon Beetner looked up from the old Nikon Super Zoom 8 camera spread out in pieces on the counter in front of him. Four children were walking into his store.

Beetner sighed, then went back to his work, carefully wiping mildew out of the camera's film chamber.

"Welcome to Beetner's Cameratown and Stuff-Yourself Teddy Bear Workshop," he droned. "You can get stuffed over there."

He flapped a hand at the far corner of the store. Two spinner racks were covered with assorted furs, all with limp arms and flaccid legs and round, staring eyes. Between the racks was a contraption that looked like an oversized gum ball machine, except that a black plastic hose hung from the side and the clear globe on top was filled with tufts of puffy white cotton instead of small multicolored balls.

Written in blocky letters along the base of the machine were the words STUFFIN' STATION.

"We're not here for stuffed animals," said one of the kids—a girl who looked to be eleven or twelve. She had blue eyes and shoulder-length blonde hair and an air of unshakable confidence people twice her age often lacked.

"Oh?" Beetner said.

Another kid—a boy who looked strikingly like the girl, though his hair was slightly darker and his face a little rounder and his expression not nearly so self-assured—stepped forward to show Beetner a disposable camera.

"There's a picture on here we need. Fast," he said. "Like, *super* fast. Like, right now, really. It's an emergency. Can you help us?"

"Can I help you?" Beetner hopped off the stool he'd been perched on and straightened up to his full six feet six inches. "*Can I help you?*"

The boy nodded—and took a cringing step back.

"Kid," Beetner said, "there is nothing I'd rather do today than help you!"

And he came around the counter with a huge grin on his face.

"Gimme, gimme," he said, holding out a big hand for the camera.

The boy looked profoundly relieved as he handed it over.

"I see a bunch of kids come in, I think, 'Great. I'm gonna sell a teddy bear today. Yippee,'" Beetner said with a roll of the eyes. He hooked a thumb at the Stuffin' Station. "I only put that dumb thing in 'cuz my wife says, 'Film is dead, Lon. Everything's digital now, Lon. You need to diversify, Lon.' But mark my words—film's gonna make a comeback. And when it does, Beetner's Cameratown is going to be ready!"

The kids looked around the store. The display cases were filled with old cameras and lenses and little boxes of film. Here and there were handmade signs.

DISCONTINUED ITEM—WHILE SUPPLIES LAST!

LIQUIDATED STOCK—HARD TO FIND!

BANKRUPT MANUFACTURER—RARE!

Everything was a little dusty and a little faded and a little sad.

"The only thing this place looks ready for," said the biggest of the kids, "is—"

He might have finished with "a broom," but it was hard to tell over the other kids' shushes. The girl elbowed him in the ribs. The littlest kid stomped on his foot.

"Ow!" the big kid said.

"Choo!" he added, fake-sneezing unconvincingly.

Fortunately, Beetner was so busy examining the disposable camera he barely noticed.

"So," the girl said to him with a strained smile, "you can open that up and develop the film?"

"In my sleep," Beetner said. "But you need it fast, so I'll do it awake. It should take me about half an hour."

"Excellent!" said the girl.

"That's great!" said the boy who looked like her.

"Thanks!" said the short kid.

The big kid was limping off toward the Stuffin' Station.

"Maybe we could stuff a bear while we wait," he said. "I bet if you pump it up enough you could make it explode!"

The girl caught up to him, hooked her arm around his, and yanked him toward the door.

"Come on," she said. "We've got another stop to make while we're over here."

As they left, she turned to throw Beetner another "Thanks!" But he was already headed for the darkroom at the back of the store, thrilled to have a new excuse to get out his chemicals and developing trays.

The other stop Tesla wanted to make was at the Wonder Hut, the hobby shop run by Uncle Newt's kinda-sorta maybe-one-day girlfriend, Hiroko Sakurai. When the kids walked in, the usually sunny Hiroko was glowering at a gangly twentysomething man standing by a stack of remote-controlled blimps.

"So this doesn't go with the models?" the man said, holding up a box with the words **MERCURY 3 REDSTONE ROCKET KIT** printed on the side.

"No, Blaine. It doesn't," said Hiroko. "That isn't just a model of a rocket. It is a rocket. So it goes with . . . ?"

Blaine blinked at her a moment.

"Uhh," he said. "The rockets?"

Hiroko tried to smile. It didn't go very well.

"Yes, Blaine. The rockets."

"Got it."

Blaine started toward the front of the store.

"Blaine," Hiroko said. She pointed toward a corner at the *back* of the store. "The rockets are over there."

"Oh. Right. Sure."

Blaine changed direction, headed up the aisle for rockets and electronics, and disappeared.

Hiroko turned to the kids and offered them a smile that was more genuine, if still a little weary.

"The new assistant manager," she whispered. "Doesn't know an ultraspeed digital gyro from a super submicro digital programmable servo."

Nick and Tesla shook their heads in sympathetic

disbelief.

Silas and DeMarco looked at each other and shrugged.

"So," Hiroko said, "what brings you in today?"

Tesla stuffed a hand into her pocket and pulled out the little black square they'd found under the seat of her bicycle.

"This," she said.

She walked up to Hiroko and gave it to her.

"What is it?" Hiroko said.

"We're hoping you could tell us," said Nick.

Hiroko gave him a quizzical look, then turned the black square over and over, examining it from every angle.

"Ah," she said.

She walked around the store's lone checkout counter and pulled out something from under the cash register.

A tiny flat-headed screwdriver.

She inserted it into the side of the black square and worked it up and down. After a few seconds, the top of the square popped off.

The kids crowded in to get a look at what it had been covering. They saw a tiny gold circuit board and green wires.

"I knew it," Nick said. "A tracking device."

Hiroko shook her head and tapped a little sliver of black mesh running alongside the circuit board.

"That's a microphone," she said.

"For, like, singing into?" Silas asked.

"No," said Tesla. "For, like, spying with."

Hiroko had questions about where the mini-microphone had come from. Even if the kids had answers, though, it was obvious Tesla wouldn't share them.

"It's just something we found," she said. "You know how our uncle's place is. Weird gizmos everywhere."

A crash and a curse came from the back corner of the store.

"Uh-oh—sounds like Blaine needs you again," Tesla said. "Thanks, Hiroko! See ya later!"

She spun on her heel and hustled from the store, the boys following right behind her.

"Do you think she was right about the microphone?" DeMarco asked when they were outside.

"Hiroko used to build robots for NASA," Tesla

said. "So, yeah, I think she knows what she's talking about."

"Why didn't you tell her the truth about where you got it?"

"Because—"

"This isn't her problem to solve," Nick cut in. "Now let's . . . oops."

He plucked the mini-microphone from his sister's hand, dropped it to the sidewalk, and stepped on it.

It crunched and crackled under Nick's foot.

"Hey!" said Tesla.

"Wasn't that evidence or something?" said De-Marco.

"Awww," said Silas. "Why didn't you let *me* stomp on it?"

Nick lifted his foot to make sure the little black square was now a bunch of little black bits.

"There was no reason to think that microphone wasn't still working," he said. "Whatever our next move is, we probably shouldn't tell the spy. Right?"

"Good point," said Tesla. She gazed wistfully at the shattered plastic and pulverized electronics components at their feet. "I think we could've come up with a more subtle way to handle that, though."

Nick shrugged, looking a bit chagrined. "I thought fast was more important than subtle. And hopefully we already have all the evidence we need anyway. Speaking of which . . ."

Tesla brightened.

"Right," she said. "Let's go see what our enemy looks like."

"Ahh—there you are!" Lon Beetner said when the kids walked back into Beetner's Cameratown and Stuff-Yourself Teddy Bear Workshop. He held up a small stack of pictures. "Just finished up. I took the liberty of printing everything on 8-by-12 glossy paper. More fun for me that way, and some of the shots you got out of that dinky little camera actually turned out great."

"Thanks, Mr. Beetner!" Tesla said, striding forward with an arm outstretched. "We really appreciate your doing this so fast."

Before Tesla could take the pictures, Beetner lifted them up over his head. He was such a tall, lanky man, they nearly scraped the ceiling.

"That'll be eighty-seven dollars and thirteen cents," he said.

"Eighty-seven dollars!" Nick said. "We don't have that!"

Beetner chuckled and lowered his arm.

"Just kidding," he said. "It's twenty-two dollars even."

The pictures were right in front of Tesla now, but she didn't take them.

"Uhh . . . I don't think we have that either," she said.

The kids started pulling crumpled dollars and loose change from their pockets.

"I've got four dollars and sixteen cents," said Nick.

"I've got three dollars and seventy-five cents," said Tesla.

"I've got a five-dollar bill," said DeMarco.

"I've got thirty-six cents," said Silas. "And some gum."

They all started toward the nearest counter, about to pile up their money by the cash register.

"Never mind," Beetner said with a sigh and a roll of the eyes. "Just come back sometime and buy a teddy bear. The markup on those things is obscene."

He held out the photographs to Tesla again.

This time, she took them.

The kids thanked Mr. Beetner, then retreated to the Stuffin' Station and began leafing through the pictures.

There was DeMarco's family by a wooden sign that read WELCOME TO SOUTH LAKE TAHOE.

There was a stony-faced Elesha standing waist-deep in crystal-clear water.

There was a scowling Monique floating in a little rubber raft.

There was DeMarco on a pebble-covered beach, grinning obliviously as Elesha sneaked up behind him with a bucket of mud.

There was DeMarco asleep in his hotel bed with LOSER written on his forehead in blue toothpaste.

Then the pictures got grayer and grainier.

DeMarco and Silas firing bottle rockets from a rooftop.

DeMarco and Silas riding their bikes with Nick and Tesla.

DeMarco creeping across Julie Casserly's lawn with a roll of toilet paper.

And then, crisp and bright and plain as day, a figure bending down toward a star-shaped pendant on a bedroom floor.

A man in a tan jumpsuit with the words VER-MINATOR PEST CONTROL printed across the back.

"Whoa," Nick gasped. "I thought for sure it was going to be Oli."

Tesla nodded.

"Me, too. But pictures don't lie," she said. "Skip didn't come to kill bugs. He came to plant them."

"The dude's been at your uncle's house all day,"

DeMarco said. "The place could be full of hidden mics by now."

"It's not just the house we have to worry about," Nick added. "I mean, if the guy took the time to put a bug on a bicycle, he could have put them anywhere."

"And he's probably not just using microphones," Tesla said to her brother. "He took that fingerprint, too, remember? How did he know where we hid it?"

Nick pondered that, then went pale.

"Hidden *cameras*," he said.

"Ew," Silas said with a squirm. "I'm never going to the bathroom in your uncle's house again."

The others ignored him.

"From now on," Tesla said, "we're only going to let Skip see and hear what we want him to, while we make all our *real* plans in secret."

"How are we going to do that?" DeMarco asked.

Rather than answer, Tesla turned to her brother with an expectant look on her face.

"We'll do it just like spies do," he told DeMarco. "We'll use code."

EGBQD OAAX CODE WHEELS

[THIS TITLE USES AN AO CODE!]

THE STUFF

- 4 Styrofoam cups (2 for each code ring set)

- Scissors

- Felt-tip marker

- The code wheel guide on page 254 of this book

THE SETUP

1. You'll need to create at least two identical sets of code wheels—one for you and one for the person you want to send secret notes to. Poke a hole with scissors below the lip of the first cup and carefully trim around the lower rim.

2. Trim the second cup like the first, but leave about ½ inch (1 cm) below the rim so that the first ring can fit over it.

trim first
cup here **1**

2 trim second cup here

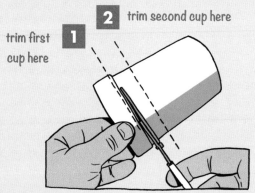

3. Working with one ring at a time, center the ring over the code wheel guide on page 254 and carefully mark the ring with a dot above each line. Be sure the ring does not move on the guide as you do this.

4. Fit the two rings together and draw a straight line down from each dot you made, as shown.

5. Write the alphabet in order on the second ring you cut, using the space between lines for each letter.

6. Repeat for the other ring. Fit the two together.

THE FINAL STEPS

1. To create a code, spin the wheels so that they line up with different letters. Each letter on the bottom ring is now represented by a new letter on the top ring.

2. Write your message in code, substituting the new letters (on the top ring) for the correct ones.

3. To tell your friend how to line up the rings to unscramble the secret message, start the code with two letters to show which letters to match up. (These are not really part of your message: for example, AO means to match the A on the top ring with the O on the bottom.)

4. If you want to make a *super*secret code, scramble the order of the letters on the top ring or use symbols instead of letters. The more complex the code, the harder it is to break!

"All right, let's test them," Tesla said when the code wheels were done. "Get out."

"What?" said Silas, surprised.

It wasn't every day he got kicked out of his own room.

"Get out," Tesla said again. "I'm going to use my code wheel to write messages to all three of you, so we can make sure you can do the translations. The test won't work if you're looking over my shoulder while I write, will it?"

"I guess not."

"All right, then. Shoo."

Reluctantly, Silas, DeMarco, and

Nick got up off the floor, where they'd been huddled around the scissors and markers and cups they'd needed to make the code wheels. It took them a while to get to the door, because they had to weave their way through a dense jungle of toys, comics, books, games, DVDs, models, moldy plates of half-eaten snacks, and piles of dirty clothes nearly as tall as DeMarco.

They'd decided that Silas's house was the safest place to build the code wheels, but that safety had come with a price: they had to work in a room that smelled like three-week-old cheese dip and sweaty socks.

The boys headed up the hall toward the equally cluttered kitchen, where Silas's mom was stirring a huge pot of soup she ominously called "Use-It-or-Lose-It Leftovers Surprise." Like Silas, she was husky and good-natured and not overly concerned with tidiness or good grooming.

"Your little club meeting over?" she asked.

"Not quite," said Nick.

He left it at that.

Silas didn't.

"Tesla made us come out here because she wants

to test the code thingies we put together so the exterminator guy hiding microphones and cameras everywhere won't know what we're doing when we go back to her uncle's house to prove that he's the spy dude her mom warned her and Nick was after them for some reason," he said.

Nick gaped at him.

DeMarco nodded approvingly.

"Good synopsis," he said.

Silas's mom chuckled.

"How do you kids come up with this stuff?" She waved her ladle at a pan on the counter, splattering the floor with drops of steaming purple liquid in the process. "Help yourselves to brownies."

"Ooo! Sweet!" said Silas.

"Thanks, Mrs. Kuskie!" said DeMarco.

They descended on the pan and began tearing out big brown chunks with their hands.

"Ready!" Tesla called from down the hall.

Silas and DeMarco walked out of the kitchen munching on slabs of brownie the size of sandwiches.

Nick didn't get any for himself. He couldn't work up much of an appetite knowing what they still had to do that day.

"Good luck catching your 'spy dude,'" Silas's mom said as the boys left. "And don't be late for dinner!"

Tesla handed slips of paper to Nick, DeMarco, and Silas.

For Nick: AP T MPE JZF QTYTDS JZFC XPDDLRP QTCDE.

For DeMarco: AH UNM FTRUX RHN PBEE YBGBLA YBKLM.

For Silas: AD VLR XOB DLFKD QL YB IXPQ.

"You each have your own unique message," she said. "Let's see who can decipher theirs first."

The boys hunkered down over their new code wheels and got to work.

"I BET YOU FINISH YOUR MESSAGE FIRST," Nick read out a minute later.

"Right," said Tesla.

"Hey!" said DeMarco.

"Just keep decoding," Tesla told him.

After another minute, DeMarco looked up again.

"BUT MAYBE YOU WILL FINISH FIRST," he read.

"Right again," said Tesla. "How's yours coming,

Silas?"

"I think I've just about got it."

Silas held up his piece of paper and read from it proudly.

"YOU ARE GOING PO BE LASP."

"Close enough," said Tesla. "We're ready."

What they were ready for, Tesla thought, was this: going back to Uncle Newt's house, making sure Skip was still there to be nabbed, and collecting the final bit of evidence they needed to prove he was up to no good.

Nick wasn't so sure they were ready. But he had to concede that he didn't have any better ideas. So Tesla's plan won by default.

As the kids walked up the street toward Uncle Newt's, Tesla noticed Nick brushing his fingers over the front of his shirt in a dreamy, absent-minded kind of way.

"You're thinking about your pendant," she said.

"Huh?" Nick looked down at the hand resting on his chest right where the pendant used to hang. "Oh. I guess I am."

"You're nervous about going back to the house without it."

Nick nodded. "Yeah. If something happens to us, there'll be no way for Agent McIntyre to track us down."

"That's why we're going to get Skip *before* something happens to us."

"Right. I know. Sure."

But Nick didn't look convinced.

The kids were all wearing backpacks now—they couldn't think of a sneaky way to carry around their code wheels without crushing them—and Tesla shrugged hers off. Without missing a step, she pulled out her code wheel and a pen and pad of paper and began jotting down a message.

It was finished just as the kids reached the front door.

Tesla showed it to Nick.

AB VD BZM CN HS, MHBJ!

The first two letters told Nick it was a B-for-A substitution code. So simple he didn't even need his code wheel to figure it out.

WE CAN DO IT, NICK!

Nick took the pen from Tesla's hand and wrote

his own message.

AB SGZMJR, SDY

THANKS, TEZ

Brother and sister smiled at each other.

Then Tesla put away the paper and pen, strapped on her backpack, and reached for the doorknob.

Gladys was vacuuming the staircase when the kids walked in. Ethel was polishing the banister.

"Hi!" Tesla said brightly. "Good job on the first floor. It almost looks like normal people live here!"

Either the maids couldn't hear her over the roar of the vacuum cleaner or they just chose to ignore her.

"Well, I guess DeMarco and I will get that snack we talked about," Tesla said for the benefit of the hidden mics and video cameras.

"Yes," said Nick. "And Silas and I will go upstairs to look for the pendants again. Gosh . . . I can't believe we misplaced them both on the same day!"

"Ha ha—what sillies we are!" said Tesla.

"Ha ha—I know!" said Nick.

"Ha ha—you're as absent-minded as your uncle!"

said DeMarco.

Silas remained silent. He'd been told not to say anything unless it was "Run!" (if someone was coming after them), "Duck!" (if someone threw or fired something at them), or "Told ya so!" (if he spotted a bald eagle—Nick and Tesla always looked skeptical when he said he'd seen them hanging around the neighborhood, and he insisted on the freedom to gloat when he was proved right).

"Do you have any more of that delicious homemade lemonade?" DeMarco asked Tesla.

They headed for the kitchen while Nick and Silas started up the stairs.

"I don't think so, DeMarco," Tesla said. "But let's go see."

When she and DeMarco reached the fridge, it wasn't lemonade Tesla was looking for. It was a little hairy body in a bowl of water.

A little hairy *brown* body in a bowl of *black-and-red-streaked* water.

"Just as I suspected!" Tesla said.

DeMarco leaned in next to her.

"Yeah?"

"Yeah."

Tesla pointed at the dead spider.

"No lemonade," she said. "Want a Coke?"

"Excuse me," Nick said as he and Silas scooted around Gladys and Ethel on the stairs.

Silas just gave each of the maids a little bow.

"Tesla and I already looked for the pendants in our room," Nick said loudly. "So I think we should search the bathroom next."

Silas simply nodded.

As the boys headed down the hall, they heard the sound of movement up ahead.

"Uncle Newt, is that you?" Nick said.

He turned into Uncle Newt's room and found what he was really looking for.

Skip the exterminator—Skip the *spy*—was stretched out on the floor peering under Uncle Newt's bed.

"All clear under there," he said when he noticed Nick and Silas staring at him. He got up on his knees and began crawling along the wall. "Now to check behind these dressers. Black widows just love hiding behind dressers."

"Have you run across my star pendant by any chance?" Nick asked. "Because that's what we're up here looking for, you know."

Skip stopped crawling.

"I thought your uncle found it," he said.

"Ah, well, he did. Kind of," Nick said. "But then I sort of lost it again."

Skip looked at Silas.

"Your friend always this forgetful?" he said with a jerk of the chin at Nick.

Silas shrugged.

"Well, we shouldn't keep you from your spiders," Nick said. "Come on, Silas. Let's go check the bathroom, like we originally intended."

Silas gave him a silent thumbs-up, and the two of them turned and sauntered up the hall as casually as they could.

When they reached the bathroom, Nick bent down and opened the cabinet beneath the sink.

"Maybe my pendant got stuck under here . . . uhh . . . somehow," he said. "I'll just take a look."

He slung off his backpack and, moving quickly and furtively, took out his code wheel, paper, and pen. Even if the house was full of hidden cameras, he figured there wouldn't be any under the sink. Who'd want to spy on pipes, spare towels, and a hair dryer?

Working with his head stuffed in next to the pipes and spare towels, Nick began writing a message.

AP DVTA TD TY FYNWP YPHE'D CZZX

"Mmm mmmm," Silas grunted.

"Almost done," Nick said.

"Mmm mmmm!"

"I said I'm almost done."

"MMM MMMM!"

"Geez, Silas!" Nick pulled out his head and shoulders from under the sink. "I said I'm—oh."

Not one but two people were looking down at him from the doorway now.

One was Silas.

The other was Skip.

CHAPTER 11

"You were right," Nick said to Silas. "The pendants are *not* under the sink. Hi, Skip. What's up?"

Skip was tilting his head to get a better look at the pad of paper in Nick's hand—and the coded message that was plainly visible on it.

"'Ap divta tud tie fyunwip yupheed cizzix'?" he said. "What does that mean?"

"Oh. Well. That. It's a . . . a . . ."

Skip untilted his head.

He was staring straight into Nick's eyes now.

"A word jumble," Nick said. "You know—one of those daily puzzles from the newspaper? This one's had me stumped all day. I can't stop thinking about it. I just love anagrams and riddles."

"So what is it today?" Skip asked.

"What is what?"

Skip pointed at the coded message.

"Today's riddle. Isn't that how word jumbles usually work? There's a riddle, and that's the answer."

"Why, yes. Yes, that is how it works. Today's riddle is . . . uhh . . . uhhhh . . ."

Nick actually hated riddles. He couldn't think of even one.

He looked at Silas, eyes wide with panic.

Silas put a finger to his sealed lips and shrugged.

Sorry, he was saying. *I'm not supposed to talk, remember?*

Nick vowed to make him say something very soon. Something along the lines of "Ouch!"

"Oh! Now I remember!" Nick said. "What's black and white and red all over?"

Skip scowled.

"*That's* had you stumped all day?" he said. "Everybody knows that one. It's a newspaper." Skip drummed his fingers on his chin. "Or a zebra with a sunburn."

"A zebra with a sunburn!" Nick cried. "That's it! It fits perfectly!"

"It does?"

Nick stuffed the paper into his backpack before Skip could look at it again.

"Yes! Excellent! Come on, Silas. Let's go tell Tesla and DeMarco we solved it."

As Nick and Silas hurried down the hallway toward the stairs, Skip stepped into the bathroom and closed the door.

Good. Let him take his time.

The man had come to the house supposedly looking for spiders. But now he was about to be caught in his own web.

Nick edited his secret message for Tesla as the two of them stuck their heads in the refrigerator talking loudly about the leftover pizza they were pretending to look for.

"I don't think Uncle Newt would've eaten the last piece. You know how he hates mushrooms," Nick said as "AP DVTA TD TY FYNWP YPHE'D CZZX" became "AP DVTA TD TY ~~FYNWP YPHE'D CZZX~~ ESP FADELTCD MLESCZZX."

Tesla used her code wheel to decipher the message, but she didn't write it down. For all she knew, there was a hidden camera in the mayonnaise. If she and Nick were being watched, the bad guys would know they were up to something, but at least she could make it hard for them to know what.

Slowly, silently, AP DVTA TD TY ~~FYNWP YPHE'D CZZX~~ ESP FADELTCD MLESCZZX took form in Tesla's mind.

SKIP IS IN ~~UNCLE NEWT'S ROOM~~ THE UPSTAIRS BATHROOM.

Perfect. It was time to act.

"Oh, well. It wasn't very good pizza anyway," Tesla said.

She backed out of the refrigerator, turned toward DeMarco, and blinked both eyes at him twice.

He was standing by the window that looked out onto the backyard. When he saw Tesla's signal—the one they'd agreed on when making their plans at Silas's house—he pretended to notice something outside.

"Hey," he said. "Isn't that a Nuttall's woodpecker

he was rarely talked about it

in that tree?"

Nick and Tesla hurried to the window and stared out in wonderment at absolutely nothing.

"Yes! It is!" Tesla said.

"Uncle Newt is going to be so excited!" said Nick. "He might not mention it very often or have any books about it around the house, but we all know how much he loves bird-watching, and the Nuttall's woodpecker is exactly the bird he's been hoping to see all summer, though he's rarely talked about it or—"

"Yeah, yeah," Tesla cut in, annoyed. She started toward the stairs to the basement laboratory. "The point is we need to get Uncle Newt up here before that bird flies away, right?"

"Right," said Nick.

He and Tesla went down to the lab while DeMarco and Silas stood stiffly by the window trying to act awed by the sight of a nonexistent woodpecker.

"Ah! The children!" Oli said when he saw Nick and Tesla coming down the stairs. He wasn't mashing rotten fruit with his feet any longer. Now he was scooping the glistening yellow-brown muck out of the tub and stuffing it into plastic bags. "It is evening, and you hunger and wonder what is for the dinner, yes? Well, you are in luck. Oli will make for you his famous Australian borscht!"

"Australian borscht?" said Nick.

"Later, Oli," said Tesla. "Uncle Newt, could you come upstairs, please? There's something we need to show you."

Uncle Newt looked up from the engine he'd been tinkering with.

"Can't it wait till after the borscht? Oh, and by the way—none for me, Oli. I'll just nuke myself a Hot Pocket."

Oli furrowed his heavy brow.

"You will do what to your pockets?"

"Please, Uncle Newt," Nick said. "It'll just take a minute."

Uncle Newt eyed the backpacks the kids were wearing.

"This isn't going to involve hiking, is it?"

"No," said Tesla. "No hiking."

"Fine. Oli, you keep bagging up that new batch of compost. I'll begin exothermic reaction tests after dinner."

"What kind of tests?" Oli said.

Tesla pointed at the muck in his hand.

"He's gonna set that on fire and see if it explodes."

"Oh."

"Boy, oh, boy," Uncle Newt chuckled as he went up the stairs. "For a guy who wants to be a M.A.D. Scientist, that Oli sure has a lot to learn. So, what is it you want to show me?"

"It's in the backyard," Nick said. "Though I wouldn't be surprised if it's moved, forcing us to chase after it."

"It's moved," DeMarco said when Nick and Tesla and Uncle Newt stepped into the kitchen. "We'll have to chase after it."

"Told ya," Nick said.

"Come on!" said Tesla.

She grabbed her uncle by one hand, Nick grabbed the other, and Silas and DeMarco swooped in from behind.

After some tugging and shoving and feigned excitement, they had Uncle Newt in the middle of his backyard.

"This far enough?" Nick asked.

Tesla looked around. The sun was setting, giving the yard a gray, gloomy look. Yet there was still enough light to see that there was nothing near-by but grass and weeds and big, black streaks of scorched earth where one experiment or another had gone awry.

Most important, there was nothing that could hide a mic or camera.

Tesla let go of Uncle Newt, and Nick did the same.

"You're not about to blow something up, are you?" someone called out.

Everyone turned to find Julie Casserly stepping out her back door, phone in hand.

"Don't worry, Julie!" Uncle Newt reassured her with a smile. "That won't be till later!"

Julie didn't look reassured. She was punching numbers into her phone as she went back inside.

"For once, I *hope* she's calling the police," Nick said.

Tesla nodded.

"Couldn't hurt to have Sergeant Feiffer around."

"Nick, Tesla—what is going on?" Uncle Newt asked.

"We'll tell you," Nick said, "if you'll just turn your back to the house and try to look like you're watch-ing a Nuttall's woodpecker."

Uncle Newt thought it over for a moment.

"Fair enough," he said.

He turned and opened his eyes wide.

"Ooo . . . what brilliant plumage!" he cooed. "Good enough?"

Nick and Tesla were already digging around in their backpacks.

"You remember that message from our mom about the spy?" Nick said. "The one that was mysteriously deleted?"

"Of course," said Uncle Newt.

"We know who Mom was warning us about," said Tesla.

She held up a small bowl she'd taken from her backpack. She'd drained the water, but a black and red residue remained—as did a little brown body with eight curled, hairy legs.

"What's that?" Uncle Newt asked.

"That's the black widow you and Hiroko found," Nick told him. "Only it's not a black widow."

"Black widow spiders don't have hairy legs," Tesla said.

"They don't?"

"Would *National Geographic for Kids* lie?" Tesla

said. "And anyway, even if black widows *did* have hairy legs, they definitely wouldn't lose their color when you soak them in water."

"You're saying that's a fake?"

"Exactly," said Nick. "The only thing we can't figure out is how it got into the house. I mean, *someone* must have planted it . . ."

Nick didn't want to come right out and suggest that it had been his uncle's special lady-friend, Hiroko. So he just let the idea hang there in the hope that his uncle would reach for it himself.

"Hmmm," Uncle Newt said. "I suppose Skip could have left it when he came in to do his sales pitch yesterday afternoon."

"Wait," said Tesla. "What?"

"Skip was here yesterday?" said Nick.

Uncle Newt nodded.

"He was going door to door talking about Verminator Pest Control."

"And it didn't seem suspicious when you found a black widow spider on your dining room table, like, an hour later?" DeMarco asked.

"Nope," said Uncle Newt. "It seemed like great timing!"

The kids blinked at one another in disbelief. Even Silas looked taken aback by Uncle Newt's obtuseness.

"Well, it certainly makes sense that it was Skip," Nick said. "Because look at this."

He handed his uncle the picture of Skip stealing his pendant.

"That was taken by a hidden camera in our room," Tesla explained. "And we found this on my bike."

She held out what was left of the mini-mic they'd shown to Hiroko. Despite what Nick's stomp had done to it, Uncle Newt recognized it for what it was.

"So Skip's spying on us. Stealing from us," he said. "Leaving spiders with bad dye jobs lying on the furniture." He pounded a fist into his palm. "Not cool!"

"You believe us, then?" Tesla asked.

"Of course! Don't I always?"

"Not really," Nick grumbled.

"Mm mmmm mm mm mm mmm?" Silas said to Uncle Newt.

"You can talk now," Tesla told him.

"So what do we do now?" Silas said again, this time with his mouth open.

"Are you going to call the police?" DeMarco asked

Uncle Newt.

"I'm not sure they'd believe *me*," he said. "I think I lost a lot of my credibility after I called about Bigfoot."

"Oh, great," Tesla groaned.

"I don't think the UFO sighting helped any, either," Uncle Newt went on. "According to Sergeant Feiffer, the police department's policy on me is 'Don't call us, we'll call you.'"

"Just our luck," Silas said. "We finally get a grownup on our side, but he can't help us because the police think he's crazy."

Uncle Newt put his hands on his hips.

"Who says I can't help? Maybe I can't call the police, but that doesn't mean I'm useless. Just try this on for size: have any of you seen a Verminator truck parked in front of the house?"

The kids exchanged puzzled glances, then turned back toward Uncle Newt and shook their heads.

"There isn't one, is there?" said Tesla.

"Nope. There's not."

"You noticed that and *still* you weren't suspicious of Skip?" Nick said.

Uncle Newt shrugged.

"I thought maybe his truck was getting a tune-up," he said. "Anyway, my point is this. It's getting dark, so Skip'll be wrapping up soon. When he goes, we need to follow him. He's obviously working for somebody. That'll be the quickest way to find out who."

"I like how you think!" Tesla declared, looking a little surprised by the words coming out of her own mouth. "We had to follow someone in the dark a couple weeks ago and we came up with a totally cool way to do it. All we'll need are a bunch of high-lighter markers, a plastic bag, some water, a pin, and about half an hour to put it all together."

"Hey!" a gruff voice barked.

Everyone looked back at the house.

Skip was leaning out the back door.

"You're spider-free," he said. "I'm leaving."

"Great! Wonderful! I'll be right there! I have some questions for you!" Uncle Newt called to him. "Thank you, children. That really was one impressive . . . uhh . . ."

"Woodpecker," Nick murmured.

"Woodpecker! Yeah, wow! Gosh oh golly, could he ever peck!"

Uncle Newt patted Nick and Tesla on the head,

then dropped his voice low.

"There's no time for totally cool. We'll have to do this the old-fashioned way. Be ready."

Then he turned and walked off toward the back door.

"What's the old-fashioned way and how do we get ready for it?" DeMarco whispered to Nick and Tesla.

They looked at each other blankly.

They had no idea.

12

Skip and Uncle Newt went inside, leaving the kids alone in the backyard. The sun was fully set now, and the sky had gone from dusky gray to nighttime black.

"I can only think of one old-fashioned way to follow somebody," said Nick.

"On horses?" Silas guessed, clearly excited by the idea despite that there were no stables nearby.

"No," Nick said. "You just . . . follow them."

Tesla nodded.

"No gadgets, no tricks. I think you're right. That's what Uncle

Newt meant. Come on."

She led the boys toward the back patio, then skirted around it, slipping into the blackness that ran along the side of the house.

"When Skip comes out the front door, we'll trail him to his car," she said.

"And then what?" DeMarco asked. "We *hitchhike* after him?"

"Well—"

Tesla was spared the indignity of finishing the sentence (which was going to end with "I don't have a clue") by the large, dark shape that suddenly separated itself from the shadows to cut them off.

"Eeee!" Nick screeched, jumping a foot straight into the air.

"Aaaa!" the shape howled back, equally startled. "Is there bear behind me?"

The shape was Oli.

He peered over his broad shoulder.

"Oh. It is Oli who scares you," he said when he saw that a bear wasn't sneaking up on him. "I am sorry."

"Why would you be scared of bears?" DeMarco asked him. "I thought you were supposed to be from

Australia."

"I am! It's just that . . . uhh . . . have you not heard of the ferocious koala bears that roam my homeland?"

"Koalas aren't ferocious," said Nick.

"They're not even really bears," said Tesla.

Oli swiped a hand at them.

"Koala propaganda," he said. "Anyhoo, as I think is said in your country, I did not come find you to discuss the man-eating mini-bears of Australia. I come on more important matter."

"Yes?" Nick said, leaning to look around Oli.

He could just barely make out the path that led from Uncle Newt's front door to the street. Skip wasn't walking along it, but he might at any second.

They had to wrap it up fast.

"I hoped to make for your dinner the Australian borscht," Oli said. "But I am finding no beets or potatoes. Even of the sour cream I see nothing. The closest I come is this Miracle Whip in your refrigerator, but I do not trust it. It sounds more like weapon than food!"

"Yeah, yeah, yeah," said Tesla, also peering impatiently at the front yard. "So?"

"So . . ."

Oli lifted something squat and cylindrical he'd been holding in his left hand.

A jar of pickles.

"This is closest I come to fresh vegetable," he said. "What do you think of refreshing pickle salad?"

"Ew," Tesla said.

The sound of voices and a door opening came from around the corner, at the front of the house.

"I mean, sounds delicious!" Tesla said.

"Yeah! Yum!" said Nick.

They took Oli by the arms and began tugging him toward the backyard.

"Why don't you start on the salad right now?" said Nick.

"You'll get to the kitchen quicker if you go this way," said Tesla.

"Oh, I see you *are* hungry!" Oli enthused. "I promise, you will not be disappointed with what I prepare! Oli's pickle salad will make the Froot Hoops and Popping Tarts in your uncle's pantry look like filth scraped from hoof of diseased cow!"

"Wonderful, great," said Nick.

"Fantastic, excellent," said Tesla.

They gave Oli a little push that sent him on his way toward the backyard. Then they spun around and hurried back to Silas and DeMarco, who were peeking cautiously around the side of the house.

"Did Skip hear us?" Tesla whispered.

"No," DeMarco said. "I think your uncle's been stalling him to give us time to get in position."

Tesla and Nick leaned out just far enough to see the front porch.

"So it's your expert opinion as an exterminator," Uncle Newt was saying to Skip, "that if I were bitten by a radioactive spider, I *wouldn't* develop the ability to crawl up walls?"

"That's right," Skip growled. It was too dark to see the expression on his face, but from his tone it was obvious he wasn't smiling.

Uncle Newt nodded gravely, as if he'd just heard disappointing news indeed.

"And I assume the same goes for super-strength?"

"Yes," Skip said. He looked pointedly at his watch. "My, oh, my—is that really the time? I've gotta go."

"But we haven't even gotten to spidey-sense yet!" Skip groaned.

At that moment, Ethel and Gladys burst out the

front door, mops and buckets in hand.

"Leaving, ladies?" Uncle Newt asked.

"You bet we are," Ethel said. "I'm about to miss the first spin on *Wheel of Fortune*."

"And if I'm not home by eight, my dogs start pooping on my bed," added Gladys.

Uncle Newt stepped off the path to let them scuttle past. Which was wise, because it looked as though the little old ladies were going to stampede right over him if he didn't.

Skip took the opportunity to make his escape with them.

"Don't forget to tell your friends and neighbors," he said as he scurried off, "when Verminator sends pests packing, they *won't* be back. Buh-bye!"

He gave Uncle Newt a perfunctory wave and practically sprinted for the street.

Uncle Newt returned the wave, then turned and went into the house.

The kids looked at one another.

"I guess it's time for some good old-fashioned following," Nick said.

"Right," said Tesla.

She led the way after Skip, bouncing like a pinball from tree to tree, hiding spot to hiding spot.

Skip and Ethel and Gladys separated without a word when they reached the sidewalk, the exterminator turning left, the cleaning ladies heading right.

The kids veered left, too, moving parallel to their quarry. They stuck to the blackest shadows as they moved—shadows that proved too black, unfortunately.

Tesla bumped into something in the dark, and it toppled over just in time to crunch beneath Silas's foot.

The kids froze.

Skip didn't. Apparently, he hadn't heard.

Before starting after him again, Nick and Tesla and DeMarco looked down.

Silas was standing on Julie Casserly's new garden gnome. Its head was now nothing but pulverized plaster beneath his sneaker.

"Oops," Silas said softly. "Maybe we can glue it back together later."

"There's hardly anything left to glue," said DeMarco.

Nick had always assumed garden gnomes would be hollow, but he noticed what looked like the broken pieces of a little black skull mixed in with the shattered plaster.

"Wow," he said. "Those things are even creepier than I thought."

"Now is not the time to be critiquing garden gnomes!" Tesla said. "Come on."

Thirty seconds later, they were watching from behind a bush as Skip stopped by a dark nondescript car, opened the door, and tossed his spray can inside.

Uncle Newt had been right: there was no Verminator Pest Control truck. Probably because there was no Verminator Pest Control.

Skip lowered himself in behind the wheel and slammed the door shut.

"So that's the guy's car," DeMarco said. "Now what?"

"I wish you'd stop asking that," said Tesla.

"I wish you'd give me an answer!"

Beside them, Silas was planting his hands on the ground while raising his butt high into the air.

"Are you doing yoga?" Nick asked him.

"No. I'm getting ready to sprint. You know, like they do in the Olympics."

"You're going to *run* after Skip's car?" Tesla said.

"You got a better idea?"

"Of course. Nick and I will go back to Uncle Newt's garage and get our bikes and—"

Skip started the car and drove off.

"Too late for bikes!" Silas said, and he took off running after Skip.

Almost immediately he tripped over a garden hose that someone had left lying out and ended up sprawled spread-eagle in the grass.

"Great," DeMarco said to Nick and Tesla. "This is what we get for listening to your uncle."

Suddenly, they heard a roar and a screech, and another car came shooting down a driveway nearby.

It was the Newtmobile—the half-jeep, half-boat, all-ugly monstrosity of a vehicle Uncle Newt had built for himself. It ran on used vegetable oil collected from restaurant fryers, which was why the smell of overcooked fast food began wafting over the neighborhood.

"Let's go!" Uncle Newt called out from behind the wheel.

"You were saying?" Nick said to DeMarco.

The kids helped Silas to his feet and then raced

to the Newtmobile and climbed in.

"Follow that car!" Tesla said.

She pointed at Skip's red taillights dwindling into the distance.

"Don't get too close, though," Nick added. "The Newtmobile isn't exactly inconspicuous."

"Don't worry," Uncle Newt said as he pulled out into the street. "Skip won't have a clue we're behind him."

The Newtmobile backfired explosively, sending a huge cloud of oily black smoke puffing out of the tailpipe.

"Ugh!" DeMarco coughed. "I feel like I'm being barbecued!"

Silas sniffed his T-shirt.

"Now I smell like french fries," he said. He sniffed the shirt again, then grinned. "I like it!"

Uncle Newt gave the Newtmobile more gas, and it roared off after the lights a block ahead.

Silas giggled and stamped his feet with glee.

"A car chase!" he cackled. "We're in a car chase!"

He and DeMarco high-fived as the taillights up ahead grew larger.

"We're coming up on him too fast," Nick fretted.

"He's gonna see us."

"I said don't worry, Nick," Uncle Newt said. "Once we're out of the neighborhood, there'll be plenty of other cars to hide behind."

"He's turning!" Tesla cried, pointing at Skip's car.

It was veering onto a side street, cutting deeper into the neighborhood.

The taillights disappeared.

"I don't understand," Uncle Newt said. "He should be heading straight for the highway. There's nothing over there but more houses."

"Whatever!" Tesla cried. "Just don't let him get away!"

Uncle Newt turned onto the same street that Skip had gone down.

There was still no sign of his car.

"Where'd he go?" Nick asked.

"Maybe he lives here," said DeMarco, checking the driveways nearby.

"Or maybe his car has, like, rockets and he took off and flew away," said Silas.

Tesla shot him a disdainful look.

"Hey," said Silas, "the guy is a spy."

The Newtmobile pulled up to another intersection.

Uncle Newt looked left.

"He could have decided to go to the highway this way for some reason," he said.

Nick looked right.

"But he didn't!" he said. "He's over there!"

Everyone followed his gaze.

In the distance were the red taillights they'd been following. Then they swung to the right and were gone again.

"What the heck is he doing?" Uncle Newt said.

"We'll figure that out later!" said Tesla. "Just go, go, go!"

Uncle Newt spun the wheel and sent the Newtmobile careening around the corner and zooming up the block.

At the next intersection, he turned again.

The taillights were in front of them again, about forty yards away.

"This Skip—if that is his real name—might be some kind of super-sneaky secret agent," Uncle Newt said, "but the man has *no* sense of direction. If he takes one more right turn he'll have gone—"

The taillights swung to the right again.

"In a circle," Nick and Tesla said together.

"Well, in a square, technically," said Uncle Newt.

When they pulled up to the next stop sign, they could see Uncle Newt's house just around the corner.

The taillights were nearby, too, though they weren't moving anymore. After a moment, they went black.

Skip had turned off the engine. He was parked about half a block from the spot he'd left just a couple minutes before.

"Why would he circle back to the house?" DeMarco asked.

"Square back," said Uncle Newt.

"Maybe he forgot something," Silas suggested.

But Skip didn't get out of his car and approach the house. They could see his silhouette in the driver's seat. Motionless.

"I think he's waiting for his boss," Tesla said. "He had to move his car just in case we noticed it before, and now he's going to rendezvous with whoever's behind all this."

"Ooo!" Silas said. "Rendezvous!"

Everyone looked at him.

"I just like the way it sounds," he said.

Everyone looked away.

"I think he might be testing his bugs," said Nick. "And if he is, he's wondering why we're not in the house."

"Good point," said Tesla.

"So what are we gonna do?" said DeMarco.

He was looking at Tesla and Nick, but it was Uncle Newt who answered.

"We're going to sneak back into the house," he said, "and then we're going to fight fire with fire."

The kids all gaped at him in surprise.

"What do you mean?" asked Tesla.

Her uncle grinned at her.

"Hey, I'm a M.A.D. Scientist, remember?" he said. "Do you really think Skip's the only one around here with high-tech spy gadgets?"

13

"Wow! Incredible!" Uncle Newt raved as he and the kids walked in the back door. "The Nuttall's woodpecker was neat, but that flammulated owl? So amazing! Thanks for showing me."

"We knew you'd like it," Tesla said.

The sound of quick, heavy footfalls rang up from the lab, and Oli burst through the door from the basement, gasping for breath. He was back in his trench coat and fedora, which couldn't have made it any easier to hurry up the stairs.

"Oh, hello! I was just down

in laboratory doing things normal interns do!" he wheezed. "Dinner is in refrigerator. I put on table for a while, but your cat keeps stealing the cheese from the pickle salad."

"You put *cheese* in your pickle salad?" Nick asked, his face going white.

"Yes! It is needing protein, so I improvise," Oli replied proudly. "And with the mustard-and-olive sauce I create, it is really quite delicious."

"Silas, DeMarco—you two love cooking," Tesla said. "Maybe Oli could show you how he made the pickle salad while we go upstairs and check on that thing we were discussing."

"What a lovely idea," DeMarco grated out through gritted teeth.

"Mm hmm," said Silas (who'd again been ordered not to talk).

Both boys were throwing resentful looks at Tesla as she and her brother and uncle headed out to the hallway. They'd known it would be their job to keep Oli from wandering into the middle of anything, but obviously they hadn't counted on doing it with pickle salad and cheese.

Nick, Tesla, and Uncle Newt kept up a stream

of meaningless chatter about flammulated owls as they went up the hall, up the stairs, and up the stepladder into the attic. That was where Skip had spent most of his day, so they didn't stop their owl-babbling even as they gathered their supplies. For all they knew, Skip could hear everything they said.

Uncle Newt dug a thermal camera out of a box marked ORTMANN EXPEDITION—LEFTOVERS. Tesla took a pair of night-vision goggles off the plastic Santa in the corner. And Nick went to get a parabolic microphone from a dust-covered shelf—and managed not to scream when he saw the giant, deformed skull resting next to it.

Once they had everything in hand, they gathered near the attic's only window. When they'd been piecing together their plan out in the Newtmobile, Uncle Newt had said it would take some work to get the window open because it had been painted shut years before. Yet with a single, one-handed push from Uncle Newt, it slid up smoothly.

Uncle Newt smiled at their good luck, gave his niece and nephew a thumbs-up, then climbed through the window to the roof.

Nick followed cautiously, making sure one foot was planted firmly in the darkness outside before daring to bring the other out with it. While Tesla waited for him to get out of the way, she noticed white flakes of paint on the floor beneath the window. Before she could bend down to examine them, Nick walked out onto the roof and waved for her to join him.

Tesla went through the window as slowly as Nick had. Their parents let them do almost any kind of experiment or project they wanted to, but one thing was always forbidden: anything to do with the roof. The one time Nick had climbed out a window to test a homemade parachute (with one of Tesla's old Barbies doing the parachuting), he'd been grounded for two weeks and lost chemistry-set and rocket-building privileges for four. Neither he nor Tesla had set foot on a roof since.

They stayed motionless, backs pressed against the side of the house, as Uncle Newt slid the window shut.

"You don't have to be so nervous," he said, voice low but not a whisper. It was pretty unlikely Skip would have bothered hiding cameras or microphones out there where no one ever went. "This part of the roof's so flat I've been meaning to put a deck up here. It'd be a great place to stargaze, don't you think?"

"Or look for UFOs," said Tesla with a roll of the eyes she assumed her uncle couldn't see.

"Oh, don't get the wrong idea about that," Uncle Newt said. "I wasn't worried about aliens. I'd spotted a literal UFO—an unidentified flying object—coming down over the state park just east of here. It looked like a meteorite to me, a big one with quite the fireball, and I was worried it might start a forest fire. But somehow when I called the police to tell them about a UFO raining fire from the sky, they got the crazy idea I was calling about an invasion!"

Tesla quietly recalibrated her assessment of her uncle's mental health. He still didn't qualify as normal, but at least he was a step closer to sane.

"Anyway," he said, "we're not out here to talk about meteorites, are we? Let's go."

Uncle Newt got down on his hands and knees and began crawling toward the roof's edge about twenty feet away.

Nick and Tesla warily did the same.

"That's close enough," Uncle Newt said, stopping them when they were only halfway to the edge. He stretched out one of his long arms and pointed at the street below. "There it is."

Nick and Tesla looked down and saw Skip's car.

It was too dark to tell if Skip was still behind the wheel . . . or if anyone was sitting beside him. So Tesla strapped on the night-vision goggles while Uncle Newt turned on his thermal camera. Nick put on the earphones for the parabolic microphone—a long-distance, handheld mic with a clear plastic dish for a receiver.

Through the goggles, Tesla could see a hazy, green-tinged image of a man sitting in Skip's car. He wasn't wearing Skip's tan jumpsuit, though. Instead, he was dressed in solid black from the chin down.

"Someone's in the car. Alone," Tesla said. "I assume it's Skip, but I don't know. If it is, he changed clothes. What do you see, Uncle Newt?"

"The heat signature of a human being," Uncle Newt reported. "It appears to be male and it doesn't seem to have a fever."

"Why do you have a thermal camera anyway?" Nick asked.

"For the same reason I have night-vision goggles and a parabolic microphone. I needed them to hunt

Bigfoot."

Tesla sighed. Just when she thought maybe her uncle wasn't *that* weird . . .

"Someone was trying to get a monster scare going out in the redwoods," Uncle Newt went on, "and I decided to set the record straight."

"So you were trying to prove there *wasn't* a giant ape-man running around in the woods," Nick said with a pointed look at his sister. He knew what her sigh had meant.

"Exactly. I collected tracks—blatantly fake—that led to that skull in the attic. Also fake. So I called the police to say that I'd found Bigfoot." Uncle Newt said, raising his hands and curling his index and middle fingers twice. "But they took it totally the wrong way. I guess that's what I get for using air quotes over the phone."

"Do you know who made the fakes?" Tesla started to say.

Nick shushed her.

"I hear something!" he said. The parabolic mic looked a little like a gun—it was mounted on a handle grip, with the dish and mic on top—and Nick used both hands to steady it. "It's Skip. He's talking to somebody."

"But there's no one with him," Tesla said. She adjusted the lenses on her goggles, and the image sharpened. "Wait . . . he's on his phone. I bet he's reporting in to his boss! Nick, what's he saying?"

Nick listened intently.

"Small pepperoni," he said. "Small Caesar salad, dressing on the side. And a Coke."

"He's ordering a pizza?" Tesla said, incredulous.

Nick nodded.

"He says he'll be there in twenty minutes."

"I don't get," Tesla said. "Why would Skip pretend to leave, just sit there for a while, and then go get dinner?"

"Maybe we can ask him," said Uncle Newt. "Look."

Through her goggles, Tesla saw a grainy-green image of Skip getting out of his car and moving quickly toward the house. He was obviously in a hurry to get away from the street and anyone who might drive by and see him.

"He's got something cold over his right shoulder," Uncle Newt said.

"I see it," said Tesla, "but I can't tell what it is."

And then Skip was gone. He was so close to the

house they couldn't see him from their position on the roof.

"What's he doing?" Nick asked.

The answer came flying out of the darkness, landing on the roof not twenty feet away.

A grappling hook.

Nick yelped, then slapped a hand over his mouth to silence himself.

For a moment, he and Tesla and Uncle Newt stared in stunned silence at the hook. Then it began to move.

Down below, Skip must have been pulling on the rope attached to it. It slid slowly across the roof until it wedged against a chimney.

"Look," Tesla whispered. "He's about to climb up here with us."

"Why would he do that?" said Nick. "He had all day to plant his bugs."

The rope squeaked as it was pulled taut, and they heard a single, muffled grunt.

"*Here he comes*," Tesla hissed.

"What do we do?" said Nick.

"Well, I don't think he's coming up here to clean out the gutters. Obviously, he's about to break into the house," Uncle Newt said. He flashed the kids a cheerful grin. "I think we ought to let him."

With a final heave, the man hauled himself onto the roof. It hadn't been easy getting up there. He'd have to cut back on the pepperoni pizzas and maybe switch to Diet Coke.

He'd worry about that later, though. For now, he had to focus. He had a mission to complete.

He moved across the roof with soft, stealthy steps. He was headed for the window he'd worked on that afternoon, carefully scraping away the paint so it would open smoothly.

When he was just a step away, he froze. He thought he heard something moving behind him, on the other side of the chimney he'd used to brace his grappling hook.

He looked over his shoulder and saw nothing but the moon hanging big and round in the starry sky.

It was probably just a bird. Probably an owl. He didn't know anything about them except that some were big and some were small and he'd run into both kinds while on nighttime assignments. And they were always annoying.

The man turned back to the window and lifted it up as slowly and gingerly as he could. One rattle or creak could ruin everything.

When the window was open wide enough, he slipped through into the pitch-black attic. He pulled his flashlight from his utility belt—he *loved* that he had a utility belt!—and turned it on.

It took only a few seconds to find his prize. He snatched it up, stuffed it into the bag he'd brought for it, and turned to go.

Mission accomplished!

He could already taste that pepperoni pizza.

He took a step toward the window—and saw three faces peering through it.

"Welcome back, Skip," said Tesla. "Not leaving again so soon, are you?"

The man was marched downstairs with his hands over his head.

"What is that thing, anyway?" he asked Uncle Newt, who was pointing the parabolic microphone at him.

"You don't want to find out," Nick told him ominously.

"He is a M.A.D. Scientist, you know," Tesla added.

When they reached the dining room, they found Oli setting the table with help from a sullen-looking Silas and DeMarco.

"We have other guest for dinner?" Oli said. "Good thing I put all the pickles in salad!"

"He won't be joining us for supper," Tesla said.

"Whoa!" Silas exclaimed, marveling at the man's all-black outfit. "Skip's a ninja!"

"Not a ninja. Just a thief," said Nick. He took the bag the man had been carrying and plopped it on the table. "And this is what he was after."

He reached into the sack and pulled out a huge skull.

"Cool!" said Silas and DeMarco.

"Ahh!" cried Oli. "What is this next to Oli's mustard-and-olive sauce?"

"It's a phony Bigfoot skull someone put in the woods to stir up publicity, for some reason," Uncle Newt explained.

Oli took off his fedora and scratched his head.

"Somehow, I still do not understand," he said.

"Me neither, actually," Nick said. "You may as well tell us, Skip. What does that skull have to do with my parents or the cameras and microphones you've been planting everywhere?"

The man lowered his hands, crossed his arms, and sneered at Nick.

"(A) My name is not Skip. That's just the name that was on the uniform I stole. And (B) I don't know what you're talking about."

He seemed to mean it.

"Oh, come on," said Tesla. "We found the mini-mic on my bike. We know you took the pendants. Who are you working for, and what are they up to?"

The man gave her a corrosive "Are you crazy?" stare.

"Why would anyone put a microphone on a bicycle?" he said. His disdainful gaze shifted to the table. "And is that diced pickles with chunks of cheese?"

"Yes!" said Oli.

"Ugh," said the man.

Oli looked crestfallen.

"All right. I think it's clear that Not-Skip here isn't going to tell us anything," Uncle Newt said. "So let's see what the police can get out of him."

He handed Tesla the parabolic mic and said, "Keep him covered." Then he walked into the kitchen and came out a second later with the phone.

He started dialing.

"Hey!" he said, surprised.

He dialed again. Then he lowered the phone.

"It went dead. No dial tone."

"Oh, geez—of course!" said Nick. "They've got control of the phone. That's how they deleted the message from Mom."

Tesla turned to Not-Skip.

"And now his boss has cut us off," she said.

The man scoffed.

"You overestimate my boss."

Uncle Newt tossed the phone over his shoulder.

"New plan," he said. "Go, go, go, go, go!"

He began frantically shooing everyone toward the front door.

"I am very confused," Oli said as he was herded along with the others.

"You and me both," said Not-Skip. "I wish I'd never taken this job. These people are nuts."

"Do you think someone's coming to get us?" Nick asked Uncle Newt.

"Well, *somebody's* been spying on us," he said. "And if it really wasn't Skip—"

"Not-Skip," the man corrected.

"Right. If it really wasn't Not-Skip—"

It was Tesla who interrupted her uncle this time.

"Then that means the real bad guys heard everything we just said."

"Exactly."

The kids started rushing toward the door even faster.

But not fast enough.

The door burst open, and a glowering Gladys and Ethel came bounding into the house. They were still in their maid uniforms, and each carried a mop that she twirled over her shoulders and around her sides like nunchucks.

"Get back," Gladys growled. "Or we'll scrub the brains right out of your head."

"Oh, give me a break," Not-Skip said.

That was a mistake.

With shocking speed, Ethel lunged forward and whacked the man upside the head with the business end of her mop.

He let out a loud "Ahh!" and stumbled sideways.

"Next time you'll get the handle," Ethel said. "Now, *back!*"

Everyone stepped back.

"What's going on?" Tesla said. "What are you two doing here?"

"They're cleaning up a mess, of course," came a cold, silky reply from outside.

Julie Casserly appeared in the doorway.

"My mess, I'm afraid. And now we're going to have to sweep it under the rug once and for all."

She stepped inside and closed the door.

CHAPTER

14

Tesla pointed the parabolic mic at Julie and her mop-wielding hench-women.

"Stay back," she said. "Don't make me use this."

Julie slapped her hands to her face and opened her eyes wide in mock fear.

"Oh, no! You mean you might *listen* to us?" she said. She dropped her hands and laughed. "You won't need a long-distance mic for that."

Tesla lowered the microphone.

Not-Skip turned to stare at it with disgust.

"I thought that looked familiar,"

he grumbled.

"Move them away from the door," Julie said to Ethel and Gladys.

The little white-haired maids stepped toward Tesla and Nick and the others, once again spinning their mops.

Their prisoners backed into the dining room in a closely packed bunch.

"Julie, is this about your gnome?" Uncle Newt asked. "If it is, I'd be happy to replace it."

"Oh, you idiot," Julie said, and she burst out laughing again. She was dressed as she so often was—in the kind of faded jeans and baggy, drab blouse she liked to garden in—yet she seemed like an entirely different woman. She'd never been nice, but now she radiated malicious, even gleeful evil.

"I already replaced the garden gnome you broke," she said. "And then your niece and nephew and their little friends went and broke the replacement just a few hours later. Lucky for me they didn't notice the camera inside it."

"Camera?" said Nick.

"Oh, yes! I've been watching you," Julie gloated. "And listening, too, of course. Just over the phone, at first. But then I decided I needed to hear more after you finally got the call we've been waiting for."

"The one from Mom," Tesla said. She was glaring at Julie so fiercely it looked as if she wanted to snatch the mustard-and-olive sauce off the table and throw it at her. "The one warning us about *you*."

Julie gave her a smug smile.

"Your parents are being extremely selfish," she said. "They know something a lot of other people would like to know. But they're not sharing, and now they're even trying to hide. Fortunately, my employers were thinking ahead. They reassigned me next to your uncle last month, and now that move is paying off. The call from your mother almost gave your parents away. We have a pretty good idea where they are now. We haven't been able to get at them yet, but when we do we're going to have a very persuasive message: We've got your kids. Now talk."

"All this fuss over how to grow soybeans," Uncle Newt said, shaking his head. "You people need to get your priorities straight."

Julie only snorted. But her reaction was enough to confirm what Nick and Tesla had long suspected.

They'd been told that their parents were horticulture experts for the Department of Agriculture, that they'd been sent to Uzbekistan to study a new method of soybean irrigation. But whatever they were *really* working on was a lot more important—and dangerous—than figuring out the best way to water beans.

"Look, lady," DeMarco said to Julie, "if you've been spying on Nick and Tesla the past few weeks, then you know they've got people looking out for them. You try anything, and Agent McIntyre is going to come busting in here with half the FBI."

"I thought she was with the CIA," said Silas.

DeMarco shushed him.

"Nice try," Julie said. "But Agent McIntyre's not going to have a clue anything's wrong until it's too late. I had Ethel fetch me Tesla's little trinket this morning. It was time I had a look at what's inside."

Julie reached into her pocket and pulled out Tesla's star pendant and necklace. One side of the pendant had been pried off, revealing circuitry inside.

"You two were right—it's a tracking device," Julie said to Nick and Tesla. "And *just* a tracking device. As long as it's in this house tonight, Agent McIntyre's going to assume everything's hunky dory."

She tossed the pendant and chain onto the table beside the pickle salad.

Nick turned to Not-Skip.

"So if you're not working for her," he said with a jerk of the head at Julie, "why did you steal my pendant?"

Not-Skip gave him a listless, chagrined shrug.

"Everyone was making such a big deal about the other pendant being missing, I figured they must be valuable. So I took one for myself. I always boost a bonus item or two. I was just hired to grab the skull— there's a certain someone out there who thinks it's real and shouldn't be hidden away in some brainiac's attic. But let me tell you, I am *not* getting paid enough for all this aggravation."

"Where is the pendant now?" Julie asked.

"In my car," Not-Skip said.

"Good. Give me your keys."

Julie held out her hand.

"Why don't you let me go out and get it for you?" Not-Skip said. "And then maybe you could just let me drive away."

"Ethel," Julie said. "Get the keys."

Ethel started toward Not-Skip, mop at the ready.

"Okay! Okay!" Not-Skip said.

He put one hand to the side of his head where Ethel had smacked him a few minutes before. With the other hand, he pulled out his keys and tossed them to Julie.

"Really, though? Why not let me go?" he said. "We're more or less in the same business. It'd be professional courtesy."

Julie scoffed.

"Our profession isn't exactly known for courtesy," she said. "Isn't that right, Oli?"

"Oli?" said Uncle Newt.

He and the kids turned toward Oli.

The big man looked profoundly ashamed of himself.

"Go ahead. Tell them," said Julie, obviously relishing his embarrassment. "You've been snooping around, too."

Oli nodded.

"I am sorry, Dr. Newt. Is true. I am spy, like these—"

He scowled at Not-Skip and Julie and her minions and said a foreign word that, though unknown to everyone present, clearly wasn't a compliment.

"But I do not want to be!" he went on. "My family owns Vakuum Vlasti. Power Vacuum, in the English. Most popular home-cleaning devices in all the former Soviet republics! When my uncle Yorgi hears that Dr. Newton Holt of U. S. of A. is working on food-powered vacuum—there was article in M.A.D. Scientist newsletter, I think—he sends me here to steal its secrets. But this is not what Oli wants to do!"

Oli gazed wistfully at the pickle salad and mustard-and-olive sauce.

"Oli wants to be nutritionist," he said.

"Wow," said Uncle Newt, looking stunned. "So I don't have a M.A.D. Scientist apprentice after all."

"Oh, but you do," said Oli. "Her name is Marta and she is to come next week. You know, your memory would improve much if you ate more fresh greens and fish rich in omega-3 fatty acids."

A loud, rough, snorting-gasping sort of sound filled the room, and everyone turned toward its source: Gladys.

She was pretending to snore.

"Oh, sorry," she said, fluttering her eyes and shaking her head as if she'd just awakened. "I must have nodded off while you folks were having your little ice cream social or whatever the heck it is you've been doing." She shot a pointed look Julie's way. "Can we knock off all the blah-blah and get this over with? My bunions are killing me."

"Yeah," Ethel snarled. "What she said."

"You two need to learn to slow down and savor these moments of triumph," Julie told them.

Gladys shrugged.

"I'd rather savor them at home with my feet soaking in Epsom salt."

"All right, fine," Julie sighed. "I'll go get the other pendant and let Control know things are ready on our end. You make sure the brother and sister are able to talk when the time comes. The weirdo, too— we might need him. The others I don't care about . . . so long as they don't leave this house."

She didn't say "ever," but her tone of voice seemed to imply it.

She spun on her heel, marched briskly to the door, and left.

"Which one of us is the weirdo?" Uncle Newt asked.

"You are," Tesla said. "You're Dad's brother. I guess they think they can use you to threaten him, too."

Uncle Newt folded his arms across his chest.

"Well," he harrumphed, "I must say I find that insulting on multiple levels."

Seemingly out of nowhere, a yowling gray shape launched itself onto the dining room table, startling everyone.

It was Uncle Newt's hairless cat, Eureka, intent on helping himself to more cheese from the pickle salad. Not-Skip used the distraction to make a mad dash for the nearest window.

Tesla was on the move, too, but not in the same direction. She was diving through the doorway into the kitchen and grabbing the phone off the floor.

She dialed 9-1.

She didn't make it to the other 1.

Gladys pole-vaulted over the dining room table with her mop, then swung it around to knock the phone from Tesla's hand. Behind her, Ethel was sending her own mop spinning across the room into Not-Skip's legs. He went tumbling to the floor; by the time he'd recovered enough to get up, Ethel was on him, vigorously mopping his head.

"I give up! I surrender! *Stop!*" he spluttered.

Ethel gave him a final swabbing across his face,

then stepped back, leaned against her mop, and admired her handiwork.

"You're cleaner," she said, "but you sure ain't prettier."

"How long do you think that Julie woman is gonna be?" asked Gladys. She wasn't giving Tesla the same rough treatment Not-Skip got, but she was brandishing her mop as if she might. "I don't like the idea of just standing around waiting for these freaks to make another break for it."

"*She's* calling *us* freaks?" DeMarco muttered.

Without so much as a glance at him, Gladys reached into a pocket of her powder-blue smock, pulled out a dry pink sponge, and threw it at him.

It hit DeMarco between the eyes.

"Ow!"

Ethel didn't even seem to notice.

"We oughta stick 'em somewhere," she said. "Lock 'em up."

"Good idea," said Gladys. "But where?"

"Oh, please—not the attic!" Nick cried. "Anywhere but the attic! I'll die of fright up there! It's so dark and icky and nasty and full of bugs!"

Ethel gave her rheumy blue eyes a weary roll.

"If you're gonna try reverse psychology, kid, at least be subtle about it." She turned to Gladys. "He wants to go in the attic."

"Obviously," Gladys said. "So we should put 'em in the basement."

"Obviously."

The old ladies began spinning their mops again.

"All right, off to the basement. All of you," Gladys said.

"And the first one to give us any guff gets their nostrils scrubbed," said Ethel.

Nobody gave them any guff. They just trooped down to the basement and let the maids slam the door behind them.

"Reverse psychology wouldn't work on them," said Tesla. "But *reverse* reverse psychology would. Nice one, Nick."

She and her brother bumped fists.

"Thanks, Tez," Nick said.

"What are you two so chipper about?" snapped Not-Skip. "Those little maniacs have us trapped in your basement."

"Wrong!" Uncle Newt grinned and spread his arms out wide. "They have trapped us in our lab!"

Silas raised his arm as if he were anxious to call out an answer in class.

"Ooo! We're gonna build something, right? I've got an idea!" He slowly lowered his arm, disappointment spreading across his face. "Only I don't know how the eagle's going to see us down here."

DeMarco gave his big friend a pat on the back.

"You just keep thinking, buddy. Quietly." He looked over at Nick and Tesla. "Do *you* have any ideas?"

Nick and Tesla scanned the laboratory for inspiration. Both of their gazes stopped on the same spot: the work table Oli had piled high with bags of freshly stomped compost.

"Oh, yeah," said Tesla. "We've got an idea, all right."

Nick just giggled.

BOOBY-TRAP BALLOON DROP

THE STUFF

- 2 small 5-ml plastic syringes (available at pharmacies)

- 1 balloon (small, water-balloon-sized ones work best)

- 1 length of fish aquarium tubing

- 1 clothespin

- Duct tape

- 1 plastic spool (from the inside of a roll of gift ribbon) with an inside diameter of about 2½ inches (6.5 cm)

- Hot-glue gun

THE SETUP

1. Remove the plungers from the syringes.

2. Attach one end of the tubing to the pointed end of each syringe.

3. Hold one syringe under a faucet, turn on the water, and slowly fill the tubing completely. Do this slowly to avoid adding air bubbles.

4. Replace the plungers, and add or remove water until pushing in one

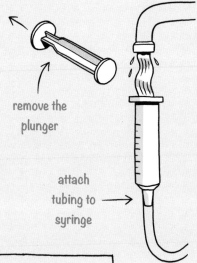

remove the plunger

attach tubing to → syringe

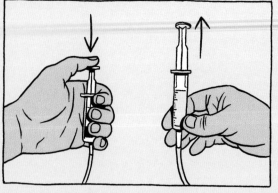

syringe pushes out the other—you're using hydraulic power!

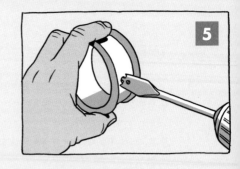

5. Remove the ribbon from the spool. Ask an adult to drill a hole in the spool about the same diameter as the syringe.

6. Place the syringe through the hole in the spool with the plunger on the inside. Hot-glue it in place from both sides.

7. Hot-glue the clothespin securely to the inside of the spool so the back of the clothespin is directly under the plunger, as shown. Adjust the plungers so that pushing on one end opens the clothespin.

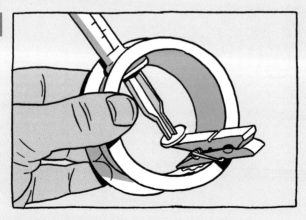

THE FINAL STEPS

1. Time to set the trap! Fill the balloon with water and pinch the knot onto the clothespin.

2. Balance the balloon on the edge of an elevated shelf so that it hangs off halfway.

3. Duct tape the spool in place.

4. Hold onto the other plunger (the one that's not pushing on the clothespin).

5. When your target is standing under the drop zone, push in the plunger.

6. Get ready to see someone look *really* surprised.

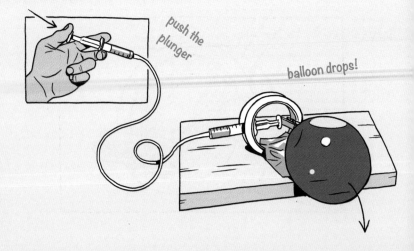

push the plunger

balloon drops!

There was some debate over whether they should use the plastic bags the compost was already in or balloons left over from an air-powered rocket car Nick had been tinkering with.

DeMarco and Oli voted for the bags because they knew who was going to have to fill the balloons with fruit sludge—them.

Nick, Tesla, and Uncle Newt voted for the balloons because they were worried the bags wouldn't burst on impact.

And Silas voted for the balloons because "Balloons, right? Ya gotta say yes!"

Not-Skip didn't get a vote.

The balloons won.

DeMarco and Oli were right about who'd fill the balloons, and Silas didn't seem to mind helping them no matter how messy and frustrating the work was at first. Once Oli hit on the idea of using a makeshift siphon—"Like for filling jelly doughnut with nourishing, sugar-free raspberry jam, yes?"—transferring the soppy, smelly glop from bag to balloon was a lot easier.

Nick and Tesla, meanwhile, worked on the hydraulic controls for the dropper as Uncle Newt quickly pieced together a radio jammer from spare electronics parts.

"Annnnnd . . . activate!" he said as he flipped on the makeshift gadget (which looked like an old transistor radio turned inside out). "If those cleaning ladies were able to sneak any bugs down here, they're worthless to them now. They won't know what's coming."

"Let's just make sure something is coming," Tesla said. "Julie could be here any second, and there's still a lot to do."

Everyone started working twice as fast. Even Not-Skip pitched in when it was time to rig the hydraulic tubes, taping them up the wall to the tilted shelf that the balloons would be positioned on, hidden behind strategically placed bric-a-brac.

"I've got a date with a pepperoni pizza," he said when Nick asked why he was helping them.

Five minutes later, Julie returned. There was no doubt it was her entering through the back door, for after a few seconds of muffled conversation she shrieked, "YOU PUT THEM WHERE?"

"Hurry, hurry, hurry!" Tesla said.

There was a burst of frantic activity as the last tubes were connected and two bulging balloons were secured on the shelf while a dozen others were tucked out of sight around the lab.

Just as the work was finished and everyone managed to strike a nonchalant pose, the door at the top of the stairs swung open.

"Didn't you read the file on these people?" Julie railed. "You don't leave them alone with technology! You don't leave them alone with a rubber band if you can help it!"

"Control doesn't let us see the files," Gladys said

petulantly. "I guess we're not important enough."

"Well, now you know," Julie snapped back. "You can't let those Holt kids or their uncle out of your sight for a second."

She came stomping down the steps but stopped as soon as she could see all her prisoners.

The booby trap was at the bottom of the stairs—still another seven steps away.

Everyone tried to appear innocent as Julie scanned the room for anything out of its proper place. But given how cluttered the lab was with miscellaneous machines, parts, experiments, and half-finished gizmos, it was impossible to tell if anything *had* a proper place.

"Listen—it's not too late to let me go," Not-Skip said as Julie's gaze swept over him. "I could be useful to you."

"You're a thief so pathetic he let himself get caught by a couple eleven-year-olds and their dingbat uncle," Julie replied coldly, not bothering to look at him again. "What use could you possibly be?"

Not-Skip licked his lips, sweat glistening on his forehead. His eyes flicked for just a second to the floor at Tesla's feet—and the trigger for the booby trap that lay there, carefully concealed behind a work table.

Nick and Tesla shot each other a panicked glance.

Was Not-Skip about to warn Julie? Had he "helped" them just so he could tell her exactly where the booby trap was and how it worked?

Even Not-Skip didn't look sure.

"Have it your way, lady," he finally said.

Nick and Tesla let out sighs of relief they hoped Julie didn't notice.

"It's almost time for you to deliver the message to your parents," she said to them. "Come upstairs, and we'll get you ready." She turned a contemptuous glare on Uncle Newt. "You, too."

"No," said Uncle Newt.

Julie narrowed her eyes.

"Excuse me?"

"No," Uncle Newt said again.

"No," said Nick.

"No," said Tesla. "None of us are going. You can't make us."

Julie narrowed her eyes even more. By now it looked like she was squinting into the sun.

"Maybe I can't. But I know who can," she sneered.

"Ethel! Gladys! Get down here!"

The maids started down the steps, mops in hand.

"The Holts are being stubborn," Julie said to them. "Show them why that's a mistake."

Ethel and Gladys squeezed past her on the stairs. As they approached the bottom, they began spinning their mops like majorettes twirling oversized batons.

Ethel reached the last step first but then pivoted to the left and hopped off the staircase early.

She didn't take the last step down to the floor. The balloons would miss her.

As Ethel started toward Nick and Tesla, Gladys copied her turn to the left. She wasn't going to step into the drop zone either.

Before she could step off, however, Oli moved swiftly toward her.

"Your little sticks and rags do not frighten me!" he declared, taking up position a few feet in front of the stair landing. "Come. Try to sweep *me* aside."

Gladys turned toward him, grinning maliciously.

"If that's what you really want, sugar," she said, "I'll wipe the floor with you."

"Hold it, Gladys," Julie said, her expression turning worried.

But she'd caught on too late. Gladys stepped off the last stair.

Tesla dropped to her knees, snatched up the syringe there, and pushed down the plunger.

Two balloons swollen to the size of melons dropped from their hiding place on the shelf. One hit Gladys squarely on top of the head. The other hit her right shoulder. Both burst, sending reeking yellow-brown pap splooshing out in every direction.

Gladys grunted and stumbled, knocked off balance, while Ethel, splatted in the back by a huge glop of compost, screamed, "I'm hit! I'm hit!"

Julie reeled back in shock but managed to keep both her balance and her wits.

"Fight, you idiots!" she bellowed at the maids. "It's just bananas!"

"And some apricots," DeMarco corrected, and he pulled another stuffed balloon out of a nearby bucket and threw it at her.

It missed. Yet when it hit the wall behind her, it still exploded in an extremely satisfying way that covered Julie's backside in goop.

Nick, Tesla, Silas, Not-Skip, and Uncle Newt were soon hurling banana-apricot balloons, too, while Oli latched on to Gladys's mop and tried to wrestle it out of her small withered hands. He was finding it harder than he expected.

"Let go, if you please, madam," Oli said as they twisted the mop this way and that. "I do not wish to harm you."

"Well, ain't that sweet?" Gladys snarled through the runny muck covering her face. "Too bad I don't feel the same way about you."

Instead of pulling on the end of the mop, she pushed, sending the handle smashing into Oli's nose.

"Oh!" Oli cried as he staggered back a step and lost his hold on the mop. "You are not nice!"

"Now you're catching on," Gladys said with a sinister smile.

She moved toward him, the mop spinning again.

Nick and Tesla tried to hit Gladys in the back with more balloons, but Ethel protected her partner by batting them out of the air. Anything thrown at Ethel got the same treatment. The floor around her was covered with fruit pulp and scraps of brightly colored rubber, but she wasn't.

The only target anyone could hit now was Julie—so that's whom they all started aiming at.

"Hey!" Julie yelled, toppling over backward as balloon after balloon splattered on her or nearby. "Ouch! Yuck! Knock it off! This isn't getting you anywhere, so you might as well stop!"

It looked like she was right. Ethel and Gladys were blocking the bottom of the stairs, and even if someone managed to get past them, Julie was splayed out on the steps drenched in slime.

And the goo-balloons were running out. Eventually, only six were left: one each for Tesla, Nick, Silas, DeMarco, Uncle Newt, and Not-Skip. (Every time Oli grabbed one, Gladys whacked it out of his hand. And now that he had no more to reach for, she was busy trying to whack *him*.)

"Wait!" Julie called out before the final balloon barrage could sail her way. "Just let me talk, would you?"

Tesla froze midthrow.

"All right," she said. "We'll listen if you call off your goons."

She jerked her head at Gladys, who was still trying to clobber Oli.

"Gladys! He's had enough!" Julie barked.

The old lady stopped lunging and thrusting with

her mop, her wrinkled lips curled in a smirk. Apparently, she liked being called a goon.

Tesla and Nick and the others lowered their last balloons.

"That's more like it," Julie said. She paused to wipe some of the glop off her face. "You know this is pointless. Your escape attempt failed. So why don't you put down those balloons and give in to the inevitable? Things might go easier for you if you do. The people I work for have been known to show mercy . . . occasionally."

"Gee, what a tempting offer," Tesla drawled sarcastically.

Beside her, Nick suddenly straightened and cocked his head slightly.

He glanced at his sister and tapped a finger against one ear.

Tesla tried to suppress a smile.

"But what makes you think this was an escape attempt?" she said to Julie.

"What would *you* call it?" Julie asked, brow furrowed.

"Well, there is a name for it," Tesla said. "Want to explain, Uncle Newt?"

"I'd love to!"

He set down his balloon and turned to a table behind him. When he faced Julie again, he had the signal jammer in his hands.

"This has been cutting off transmissions from the house for the past ten minutes," he said. "All your bugs have been blocked."

"So?" Julie said.

"So," said Uncle Newt, "it's not only the mics and cameras that haven't been sending a signal."

While Uncle Newt let that information sink in, a sound in the distance grew steadily louder. The sound Nick had noticed a moment before.

The sound of sirens.

Julie finally heard it, too. The parts of her face that weren't coated in banana gunk went chalk white.

"What's going on?" Ethel asked her.

"Our pendants—the ones with the tracking devices inside?" Tesla said. "Julie brought them back into the house. So when Uncle Newt turned his signal jammer on, Agent McIntyre lost contact with us. She wouldn't know what was going on, but she'd know *something* was wrong, and—"

"She'd call the cops," Gladys finished for Tesla,

spitting out the words so bitterly it was a wonder her dentures didn't fly out with them.

"Exactly," Tesla said. "So our little ambush was what's technically known, I believe, as a delaying tactic."

"Or a diversion," Nick said.

Tesla frowned at him.

"I think delaying tactic captures it better."

"But without a diversion we couldn't have—"

"Aw, shut your traps, ya wisenheimers," Gladys cut in. "Come on, Ethel. Time to blow."

Both old ladies spun on their heels and started to stomp up the staircase. Julie tried to get to her feet and beat them to the top, but so much slime coated the steps that she couldn't get any traction.

"Seems like a shame to let these go to waste," DeMarco said, giving his last balloon a little waggle.

"So let's not waste 'em!" Tesla said with a grin.

She and her brother and their friends took aim, and seconds later six sludge-swollen balloons—one red, two green, three blue—flew through the air. Knocked off balance by one crud bomb after another, Julie and her cronies slid down the stairs, ending up in a sodden, putrid pile on the basement floor.

Not-Skip walked up to them and gazed down at Julie, shaking his head sorrowfully.

"Oh, look—a spy who let herself get caught by a couple eleven-year-olds and their dingbat uncle," he said. "How pathetic."

Julie growled and made a half-hearted swipe at his ankles.

Not-Skip hopped back and clucked his tongue at her.

"Now, now. Better be on your best behavior," he said. "We're in enough trouble as it is."

He nodded at the top of the stairs.

Sergeant Feiffer of the Half Moon Bay Police Department was gaping down at the strange, messy scene at the bottom of the stairs: a ninja taunting Newton Holt's neighbor, who was on the floor under two maids covered in rotting fruit pulp and burst balloons. A California state highway patrol officer peered over the sergeant's shoulder with wide, disbelieving eyes.

"Why do I get the feeling it's gonna take me a looooooooong time to write up this report?" Sergeant Feiffer said.

"Remember when we didn't know what the inside of a police station looked like?" Nick asked his sister.

"I think so," said Tesla. "It seems like a million years ago."

In fact, it had been just two weeks.

Since coming to live with their uncle, Nick and Tesla had been to the Half Moon Bay police station three times.

Sergeant Feiffer was putting the finishing touches on their statement (also their third in two weeks) as they talked. He was a mild, balding man with a fondness for the kind of short-sleeved work shirts and wide ties that had gone out of fashion twenty years before Nick and Tesla were born.

"And there we go," he said, clicking **SAVE** and looking up with a smile. "You know, I always thought I might try to write spy novels when I retire. You two have been giving me lots of practice."

"What comes next this time?" Nick asked.

Sergeant Feiffer shrugged.

"You got me. Julie and those maids aren't talking. I can't even get their real names out of them. And they aren't screaming for a lawyer like most of the people who end up in a cell. It's like they're just sitting there waiting for something."

"Well, do us all a favor while they wait," Nick said. "Don't let those old ladies anywhere near the cleaning supplies."

When Sergeant Feiffer walked Nick and Tesla out to the police station's small lobby, Silas was already gone—picked up by his parents ten minutes before. DeMarco, Oli, and Uncle Newt were still there, though, saying their goodbyes to Not-Skip.

"Thank you for not you-know-what," Not-Skip was saying as he shook Uncle Newt's hand.

"I thank you, too," Oli chimed in. "You are good man."

"You-know-what" meant "pressing charges."

Both Oli and Not-Skip looked a lot more comfortable when Sergeant Feiffer turned to go back to his office.

"Sure you won't tell me who hired you?" Uncle Newt asked Not-Skip.

The man shook his head.

"There really is some honor among thieves, you know. But I can tell you this: whomever she hires next to go after that thing in your attic, it won't be me. From now on, I'm steering clear of Half Moon Bay!"

With that, Not-Skip turned and hurried away.

"'She'?" Uncle Newt mused as he left.

The door hadn't even fully closed behind Not-Skip when DeMarco's parents came charging through it, little Elesha and even littler Monique in tow.

"I—" DeMarco said.

"Don't give me that!" his mother thundered. "I don't want to hear it!"

"But—"

"No excuses, young man!" his father boomed. "You are in a world of trouble!"

"If—"

"Outside! To the car!"

"Right now, young man!"

DeMarco gave his friends a look of sheer misery and started trudging toward the door.

Tesla took a step after him.

"Mr. and Mrs. Davison," she said, "I hope you'll keep in mind that your son was only trying to help friends in trouble."

"It is our opinion that certain friends are in trouble altogether too much," Mrs. Davison sniffed.

"And the kind of help they need, a twelve-year-old shouldn't be giving," Mr. Davison added.

Each parent put a hand on DeMarco's back and steered him toward the door.

"Oh, don't forget to pick up the D-Rocket!" Nick called after them.

Mr. and Mrs. Davison stopped and glowered down at their son.

"We had to leave my bike behind a Dumpster this afternoon," he explained. "It kind of broke in two."

His parents looked at each other, shook their heads in a "Where did we go wrong?" kind of way, and began guiding DeMarco away again.

As they left, Elesha and Monique paused just long enough to look back, mime mocking laughter, and then stick out their tongues.

"What unpleasant little girls," said Oli. "Perhaps they need more magnesium in diet."

A moment later, he and the Holts were leaving the police station, too.

"So, what's next for you?" Uncle Newt asked him.

"I am not excited about flying home to tell Uncle Yorgi I do not steal your design for vacuum cleaner. So maybe I stay in America a while. I already do with the Google and find many fine undergraduate programs for nutrition science."

"That's a great idea!" Uncle Newt said, slapping Oli on the back. "Get some more science in you, and maybe you could come back as my *real* apprentice one day. You're the best banana masher I've ever seen!"

Nick noticed that Tesla seemed distracted while Oli and Uncle Newt were talking. He followed her gaze and saw a familiar black SUV parked up the block.

"So that's what Julie and Ethel and Gladys have

been waiting for," he said.

Tesla nodded.

"It's not Sergeant Feiffer they have to worry about," she said. "It's *her*."

One of the SUV's back windows rolled down, and a woman with short red hair and a pale, grave face leaned out.

"Got a minute?" Agent McIntyre said.

When Nick and Tesla climbed into the SUV, they found they weren't alone with Agent McIntyre. A gray-haired man in a black suit sat behind the wheel. He didn't even look back at the kids as they scooted in behind him. He just stared straight out through the front windshield as if he was a mannequin propped up in the driver's seat.

"I hear you've had quite a day," Agent McIntyre said to the kids. "Wanna tell me about it?"

They did. Tesla did most of the talking, though Nick contributed whenever he felt she'd skimmed over something too quickly. They both talked fast, though. They had an important question to get to.

"Are our mom and dad all right?" Nick asked

when the story was finished to his satisfaction.

"Julie made it sound like the people she works for were about to get them," Tesla added.

"Don't worry about your parents," Agent McIntyre said. "Things got a little . . . stressful, but everything's under control now. Our enemies tipped their hands today. That's going to help us in the long run."

"The long run?" Nick said. "How long is that gonna be?"

How long before we see our parents? he meant. *How long before our family is together again?*

"I'm sorry. I don't know the answer to that," Agent McIntyre said.

"Why are people like Julie after Mom and Dad in the first place?" Tesla asked.

The pinched, pained look on Agent McIntyre's face made it plain that was the one question she *really* didn't want to be asked.

"*Please* tell us something," Nick said. "Our lives have been turned upside down. If there's a good reason, it'd help to know it."

"Well . . ."

Agent McIntyre looked at the man in the front seat.

"They're intelligent children, and the theories have been a matter of public record for years," he said in a deep, dry voice. He spoke without so much as glancing into the back seat or even moving a single muscle other than his mouth. "If they want to look up SBSP when they get home, it wouldn't do any harm."

"SBSP?" Tesla said. "You mean space-based solar power?"

"Laser-beaming energy to Earth from giant satellites?" said Nick. "We had no idea Mom and Dad were working on something so cool!"

The man finally looked back at the kids, cocking an eyebrow in surprise as he examined them in the rearview mirror.

"You *are* intelligent children," he said.

Nick shrugged. "We watch a lot of PBS."

"But I don't get it," said Tesla. "SBSP is just a fancy way to generate a lot of solar power. Why all the lies and secrets and spies?"

"If you could beam thousands of megawatts to Earth from orbit, you could use it to power entire cities," the man said. "Or . . ."

Again he turned his gaze away, staring blankly

ahead into the darkness.

"Wrap it up, agent," he said. "There's been enough chitchat."

Agent McIntyre slipped a hand into the inside pocket of her suit jacket.

"I have something for you from your parents," she told Nick and Tesla. "New and improved."

She pulled out two star-shaped pendants hanging on thin chains. Gold now instead of silver.

"More tracking devices?" Tesla asked as she took one.

Agent McIntyre gave her a tight, cryptic smile.

"Sort of," she said. "Wear them close to your hearts."

"We will," said Nick.

He and Tesla put on their new necklaces and tucked the pendants under their shirts.

"Well," Agent McIntyre said, "I've got business to attend to inside. A transfer of custody from the Half Moon Bay Police Department to . . ." She flashed the kids another of her little enigmatic smiles, and her eyes darted toward the man in the front seat. "A higher authority."

The door Nick and Tesla had come in through

popped open on its own.

"Oh. Okay, then," said Tesla, getting the not-so-subtle hint. "Bye."

She and her brother started to slide out of the SUV.

"Goodbye. You two stay out of trouble, now," said Agent McIntyre.

"We will," Nick told her.

"Somehow," said the man in the driver's seat, "I doubt that."

When both Nick and Tesla were out on the sidewalk, the door slammed itself shut.

There are times when siblings can communicate without saying a thing, and this was one of them. Nick looked at Tesla, Tesla looked at Nick, and there was no need for words.

They knew what the man in the SUV had been hinting at—and why it made them very, very nervous.

Yes, the orbiting solar energy system their parents had been working on could be used to power entire cities.

Or it could destroy them.

Uncle Newt and Oli were waiting patiently by the Newtmobile while the kids had their talk in the SUV. When Nick and Tesla rejoined them, Uncle Newt slapped his hands together and rubbed them back and forth with glee.

"You know what I'm in the mood for?" he said.

"Food," Nick and Tesla said together.

It wasn't just the third time they'd been to the police station. It was the third time they'd been there with Uncle Newt. They knew by now how excitement affected him.

"I'm pretty sure there's gonna be an unclaimed pepperoni pizza waiting at Ranalli's Italian Kitchen," Nick said. "Maybe we should go get it."

The idea had Uncle Newt practically dancing a jig with joy.

"Maybe with stromboli and garlic bread and chicken vesuvio?" he said.

There was a rumbling, gurgling growl nearby.

It came from Oli's belly.

"Excuse me," he said, his broad face turning red. "We never got to sit down for pickle salad, and by now I am sure your cat has licked the bowl clean."

"You should come along, then," said Nick. "Would that be okay, Uncle Newt?"

"Of course! I'll call Hiroko and tell her she should come, too."

"Silas never got any dinner either," Tesla pointed out. "Maybe you could call the Kuskies and see if they want to meet us at Ranalli's."

"Great idea!"

As Uncle Newt pulled out his cell phone, the little group started walking up the street toward the restaurant. Nick and Tesla glanced at each other and exchanged small, sad smiles. Once again, they were speaking without words.

It's scary not knowing when our family will be back together, they were saying, *but it's nice knowing there's something like a new family we can be part of in the meantime.*

Oli noticed the kids' melancholy looks and slapped his hands onto their backs.

"Why looking glum?" he said. "The evildoers are in jail, and we are going for pizza and perhaps visit to one of these wondrous salad bars I have heard tales of. You should be happy, like Oli!"

"Oh, we are," said Tesla.

"See?" Nick said, pointing to the big grin he was giving Oli. "No more glum."

But the grin flickered and faded a minute later when Nick noticed Tesla giving the starry sky above them a long, brooding look.

Somewhere up there right now, skimming along the edge of space, might be the invention that had taken their parents from them. And it was only a matter of time before it brought them more trouble down on Earth . . .

Here's the Template for **Nick and Tesla's** EGBQD OAAX Code Wheels (page 151)

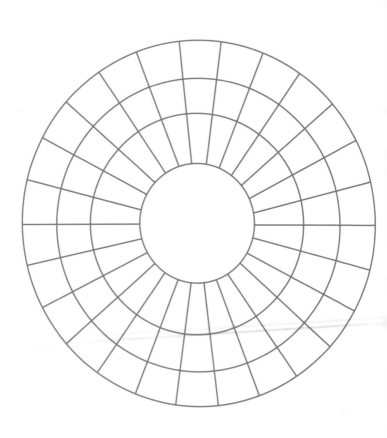

About the Authors

"SCIENCE BOB" PFLUGFELDER is an award-winning elementary school science teacher. His fun and informative approach to science has led to television appearances on the History Channel and *Access Hollywood*. He is also a regular guest on *Jimmy Kimmel Live*, *The Dr. Oz Show*, and *Live with Kelly & Michael*. Articles on Bob's experiments have appeared in *People*, *Nickelodeon* magazine, *Popular Science*, *Disney's Family Fun*, and *Wired*. He lives in Watertown, Massachusetts.

STEVE HOCKENSMITH is the author of the Edgar-nominated Holmes on the Range mystery series. His other books include the New York Times best seller *Pride and Prejudice and Zombies: Dawn of the Dreadfuls* and the short-story collection *Naughty: Nine Tales of Christmas Crime*. He lives with his wife and two children about forty minutes from Half Moon Bay, California.

FOR MORE
ELECTRIFYING Fun,
VISIT

NickandTesla.com

- Discover instructions for bonus gadgets!

- Watch videos of super-cool science experiments!

- Read an interview with the authors!

- Get exclusive sneak previews of future Nick and Tesla mysteries!

- Share photos of your own electronic gadgets and creations!

- And much, much more!